Praise for Jim Krueger

"Jim Krueger is one of the best writers there is."
–*Sam Raimi*; Director, *EVIL DEAD* series, *SPIDER-MAN* and many global cinema hits.

"As a consummate storyteller, Jim Krueger cajoles and conjures, shocks and soothes, glides and guides, and the reader can just sit back and get swept away. Jim's life is story, and that is clear with every word on the page."
–*Todd Komarnicki*, Novelist; Producer of the Christmas blockbuster, *ELF*; and screenwriter of such hits as SULLY.

"This collection of charmingly strange Yuletide treasures showcases Jim's uncanny ability to take stories and themes we thought we knew and completely redefine them, injecting them with heart, depth, and more than a little darkness. The tales contained herein will plunge you deep into the unexplored corners of the Christmas season."
–*Patrick McHale*, the creator of *OVER THE GARDEN WALL* animated series, and writer of Del Toro's *PINOCCHIO*.

"Jim Krueger guts himself and spills his soul onto the pages in an act that helps me find my own soul again. He reminds us that hope is real, hope is empowering, but hope is not cheap."
–*Doug Jones* (star of HELLBOY, PAN'S LABYRINTH, SHAPE OF WATER)

I Saw Mommy Killing Santa Claus and other Cursed Christmas Stories

By
Jim Krueger

12 Stories

I Saw Mommy Killing Santa Claus
and other Cursed Christmas Stories

All Rights Reserved

ISBN-13: 978-1-925956-97-9

Edited by Jaime Jameson
V1.0

IFWG Publishing International
Gold Coast
www.ifwgpublishing.com

Table of Contents

Introduction

An Author's Justification At Christmas, Once Again…

If you picked up O' Haunted Night Book One, you already know my love of Christmas and monsters. Of blessings and beasts. Of holidays and horror. Of the darling and the damned. And, of course, stocking stuffers, whether there is still a severed foot in the stocking or not.

O' Haunted Night Book One, *The Frankincense Monster and Other Creepy Christmas Stories*, included thirteen haunted Christmas stories, all of which were my own nightdreams and daymares regarding different aspects of the holiday. Not all of them were happy, not all ended well for the characters, but that's this time of year. And not everything is merry for all. This book includes the next 12 in what I hope will become its own Christmas tradition. Think of it as an Advent Calendar of Holiday Horror for the whole family. Well, most of it at least. Or those willing to stay up late enough on the 25 Eves of December to partake in the myths and the monsters and the, at least sometimes, merriment.

To begin…

I know and I believe that there are curses in this world. Some curses come as consequences to choices. But some choices are also the result of curses. We talk about free will as if it were a certainty, an almost primal guarantee to life. I'm not saying it's not true. but isn't it more of a mystery, nuanced by geographical and geological and generation considerations? Or is Free Will something we take on faith as much as we do anything else?

Are there not those moments when we confess to ourselves, and perhaps even to others, that we had no choice in a situation. No choice at all. Or that if we had known what would have come from a decision, we never would have chosen it at all?

Our choices and our curses, they make us, they forge us, and, like certain ghostly chains, fasten us to an impossible destiny. One that sometimes leads us to beg, in the hollows of a cold eve, for something more. And that more is something filled with newness and kindness, even if just for a moment's warmth. Like a match struck in a cold alley that will burn only long enough to show us the door to another world.

Isn't that what Christmas is? That little piece of struck coal that warms and brings light and promises to something that can't even be imagined… but still leaves a shadow to haunt each one of us until the next year brings that spark back to our lives.

I say that Christmas is this spark. It is our soul's defiance to the world as it is. Or was.

Before anyone can say let there be light, there must be a "let there not be darkness."

Even if it is only a thought or the slightest whisper.

It's not just gifts that are put into boxes this time of year, or all times of the year, for that matter. There are expectations of who we ought to be or are. Expectations of what to expect from each other. What to believe. Who to vote for. How to exist. In so many ways, we all live and walk around the world in these boxes of expectation. And these boxes, for better or worse, are their own form of curses.

Without exception.

Except at Christmas.

A cry in an old barn is eventually heard around the world and tells those in power that the way things are is not the way things must be.

Or a concentrated piece of coal on a ring changes a destiny promising someone who has always been alone that they will be alone no more.

Or the night showers ice upon the world reminding all that amid the storm, beauty is to be found. A beauty that even reflects the light of the furthest stars but even allows the deadest moon to seemingly beam with new life again.

We need our hope. In the darkness. In the storm. In the confines of our own boxes. Or coffins as might be the case in some of these stories.

Is that not the hope we are hanging on, like an ornament on the branch of a dead tree that still pretends or believes it can show new life?

I think so.
I believe so.
I hope so.
I wish so.

Jim Krueger

I Saw Mommy Killing Santa Claus

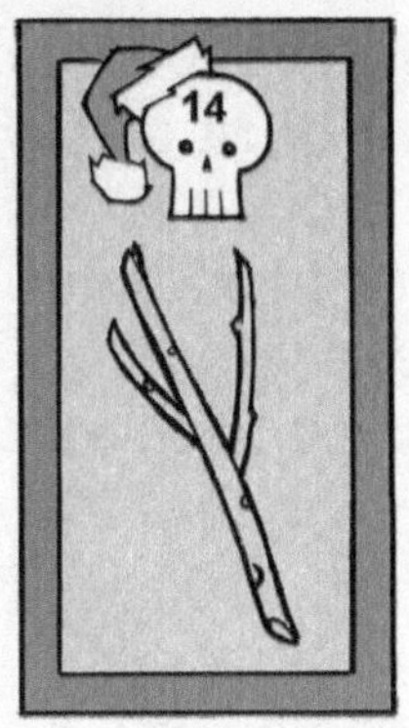

I hate lies.

Even, or maybe especially, the so-called good ones. You know, the ones that are told to make you feel better or give you hope. The ones someone tells you because they think you are not ready for the truth yet. Or that by deceiving you, they are doing you a true kindness.

I used to think that there was nothing worse than a fake Santa until the real one showed up. But I'm getting ahead of myself, just like all the stores that start trying to sell you Christmas trees before it's even Halloween yet.

As I said, I have a problem with lies. I have a problem with fakeness. And especially false promises. Which is why, maybe, Santa is one of the worst. Because the lie affects culture. And generations. Kind of all of reality after Thanksgiving. Maybe even Halloween as certain writers seem obsessed with mixing horror with the holidays. They'll tell you about the centuries-old traditions in England of telling ghost stories the night before Christmas. They'll go on and on about how this tradition dated well before Charles Dickens.

Anyhow, back to Santa.

Whether it was those department store Saint Nicks with their fake bungee-beards and self-justified-pre-or-post-diabetic-candy bellies or the bell-ringing do-gooders with a brass band behind them, I hated them. I really did. They pretended to be something they were not, and everyone cheered. And encouraged them to keep on lying. To keep on ringing that bell.

And I know, I know that they represent a story and the spirit of a story and that it's all in the so-called Christmas spirit of the thing. I know. And maybe I could forgive that.

But what if it was the real Santa that was threatening your life… as in trying to kill your mom? Trying to take what little you have left of a family? Wouldn't you agree that that was worse? Wouldn't you agree that a certain something was lost in the so-called 'spirit' of the thing?

This is my story.

And by story, it's a true one, no matter what my mom might tell you. I think she's trying to change the story a bit to let me still enjoy Christmas. She still wants me to believe in things. And I do. Just not the things she wants me to.

But after what I… what we went through this last December, I am more than fine if my mom is the one that buys me my presents. Mommy Christmas is just as good as a Merry Christmas in my book.

I'm all for peace on Earth and all that. Except for maybe the North Pole. No peace there, I hope. It's probably the doorway of Hell. No wonder it's melting.

And Santa misspelled is Satan. Or maybe it's Satan that's misspelled.

Of course, I never believed Santa would be like this when I was young. I accepted the big fat lie, with an emphasis on fat. I thought that it was okay for him to watch me when I slept or that it was a good thing at those times when I was most vulnerable, for him to watch me while I wept.

I really believed this. I really did. I thought that privacy was not an issue when it came to Santa because he kept us safe. I thought he knew all and it was important that he did.

But that was before… well, I guess I should let you know that… I guess it's important to know that I haven't had a Dad for a long time. It doesn't mean he died. It just meant he wasn't here. He left. Another lie. One that said that he would never leave. Never leave me. Or my mom.

It sort of changed the way I looked at the world.

When I first heard that song about Mommy kissing Santa

Claus I was immediately horrified in thinking that the song's Mommy was cheating with Kris Kringle, who was also married by the way. Because we all know that there's a Mrs. Claus. I think that's when I started to think about what he was actually doing visiting every house in one night. And exactly what kind of 'cookie' he was actually searching for. And we all know that Santa didn't need to buy the cow because he was getting the milk for free. House after house. Chimney after chimney.

Eventually my mom explained the song to me, but it didn't matter. I could see that she was concerned about what I was thinking about and even tried to say some nice things about my dad.

The one who left.

And then there were the stories of Santa not existing. The ones you hear from other kids who said it was really their dad. Well, for me, at this point, it was like my dad didn't exist either.

And it kind of got me thinking that I didn't have to be nice anymore. I could be naughty. I could cry or even make others cry and no one was watching. Not really.

I started getting in trouble at school and my grades started going down. I did a bunch of other things that my mom didn't like either, whether she found out about them or not.

Which brings me to this last year's Christmas. My mom went all out this last year with decorations. She even had a lighting company come to our house to make our place look like we loved Christmas more than anyone else. So that we would be the brightest house on the block. There were also as many lights inside as there were outside.

There was a Christmas tree on every floor of our home, including the attic and the basement, which really didn't make a lot of sense. All were freshly cut and still oozed the sap that can only be the sap of the holidays. It just felt like she was perpetuating another lie. This one being that Christmas made a difference.

She had also inherited, or is that been dumped upon, a Nut-cracker collection from this also-a-nut occultist friend of hers, and the nutcrackers were lined up like soldiers throughout the house. Each had something called a Bat Nut in its wooden jaw. I asked about these things, also called Devil Pods, and all my mom said was that it was a tradition and a way to ward off evil spirits.

Candles that smelled of either pine or cookies were lit everywhere. She had created a playlist of her favorite Christmas songs. It was overkill, but she insisted that the house be filled with the spirit of Christmas.

I asked why.

She said that it needed to be. And spoke of something else the nut-ball friend who died had left her. Something about a warning. Something cryptic about needing to prove something or other… but I had stopped listening by the time she got to it.

The point was that everything was Christmas. Every smelly melodic blinking thing was Christmas.

Everything but me, that is.

But in all fairness, she was not joyful either and seemed worried.

There was a rocking chair in the main family room. She had dragged it in. Mom sat in it, rocking quietly, as if even the creak of the chair were something that might conflict with the nauseating repeated crooning of a Perry Como Christmas. Mom had a rifle in her hand. And was sucking the tips of candy canes down to a point.

My mom sat in the chair as if she were on guard. But there was nothing to be on guard for. Nothing but a chimney which already had a fire in it.

Sick of it, I went to bed. And eventually fell asleep.

Later that night, while I slept and dreamed of the freshmen whose lives I would torment once the holidays were over, I awoke to the sound of hooves on the roof. But it wasn't the sound of eight tiny reindeer. It was like Hell had landed with a single set of hooves.

It wasn't bells that I heard, it was the clanking of chains. It was the dragging of iron. And when I first heard what sounded like an attack on the chimney, it sounded like a cruelty. It wasn't natural. It was like the bricks themselves were crying out to be saved.

Something was breaking its way down into the chimney. It was as if there were a terrible hollowed anger in the walls that was threatening to break down into my room.

It was at this moment that I began to feel a terrible dread.

Whatever it was, it had stepped from the roof and was moving down through the chimney, and it was headed down.

Down.

Down.

Down.

Into my house.

And I had left my mom to deal with it. With her gun. And her pointed Candy Canes.

And all her stupid Christmas symbols.

She believed in the holiday, I did not.

She hoped for me, I did not.

The first thing I heard was the end of the creaking of the rocking chair. She stopped creaking in the moment that Santa started making his way down the chimney.

I should have gone downstairs. I should have. I waited like the coward I was. I heard the rifle. She cocked it. It went off. I heard the second shot. She reloaded. Two more shots followed. And then my Mom started singing. Joy To The World. But it was so aggressive. Not like joy in a normal way, but like an anthem meant to damn the undead.

And then Santa started to speak.

He was condemning me. Cursing me for hating Christmas. Cursing me for the bad things I had done and what was in my heart. The idea of coal was mentioned and Santa believed that coal, usually given to warm a cold heart, which is why it was given, would not make a difference in my case.

She told him that he was wrong. That I had worth. That his Naughty List meant nothing to her. She was a mom and she knew better. Far better. And saw better than he ever could. She saw when I was good, which was almost never in all fairness, or when I cried, or when I slept or was awake. She saw it. She knew it. As only a mother could.

I heard her mock Santa as I assume he showed her his list. It sounded like he showed her the sack he carried for my condemnation, and she defied him and shot him again.

She reloaded and shot again. And then I think she stabbed him with a couple of those candy canes. All I know is that she must have made a hole in that sack of his. He screamed at her for that.

There was no mouse that could have slept through this. No creature that wouldn't stir. Or run for its life. Except for me, I suppose.

I cowered under my covers. And just hoped and waited that it would all be over soon.

There's something about bullies. People like me. We're cowards. But there was also something in me that refused to let her fight Santa all on her own.

So when I finally stepped the steps that guided me downstairs the next morning, I found the red or blood-stained eyes of my mom looking at Santa. She was crying. She was not going to let Santa have me. Or take me. Even if she had to get into the sack herself.

She took one more shot at Santa, whose face I never saw, and he exploded into smoke. Smoke that smelled of burned coal.

The living room had never looked worse. It still smelled like pine and cookies, but now it also smelled like gunpowder and burning things.

I stepped down into what now seemed like a war zone and my Mom rushed forward to hug me. She cried still and called me her good, good boy. She was lying, of course.

I asked why Santa disappeared.

She told me that that wasn't Santa at all. But I'm pretty sure she was lying. Though she did say it was a Krampus, one of those dark shadows of Santa, who, when a child really hates Christmas, comes and takes the child away until, in the darkness and confinement of the sack, the child learns how to love Christmas again. Which is why she poked some holes in the sack. To make sure, even if she lost, that light could get in.

To be fair, there's no such thing as a Krampus.

This was Santa, clearly, who was especially angry that I still refused to believe in him.

But after this, I think I believed in my mom more than ever. Even if she was lying to me. One of the good ones. One of those lies intended to do good.

My Mom whom, I guess, I should make more of an effort to be a little better for. Maybe it's enough at Christmas just to say "I love you" to those that you do.

THE LIST

To even mention a list around the holidays is to suggest a certain infamous categorizing of the good and the bad, the nice and the naughty, and even the sleeping and the awake. But this list is clearly not the only list one thinks of during the times before and immediately after Christmas.

Sometimes there is a list for recipients of a holiday greeting or a gift. Or a form letter that can either be appreciated or ignored or be a frustrating slog to read through. This list is usually based on the number of loved ones in a person's life, though in many cases this list expands the closer one gets to Christmas. And this expansion is usually the result of the guilt one feels of receiving a card from someone you didn't plan on sending one to. This also serves well to keep the Postal Service, created by Ben Franklin incidentally, in business.

There is also the list of things to do before a holiday break before any holiday time can be taken off. It's usually a list of tasks and preparations.

Or there is the list of events to be enjoyed around the holidays. This includes the parties and the get-togethers and the charity events and the galas.

And it is this kind of list that brings mention to the infamous Lady Alala Cassandra.

Alala Cassandra is a true mystery.

A true mystery woman.

Though there have been some pictures supposedly taken of Alala Cassandra, it is said that no one has ever seen her face to face. This, of course, is untrue. But it adds to the mystique of the famous artist and her almost rabid fandom. She is, perhaps, the most influential influencer to all those who would be considered in the upper fraction of the one percent.

And so it was that this year, she decided she would have a holiday party. Her first. Perhaps her only. No one really knew how old she was. Because of the nature of the lack of pictures, her age was always speculated upon, as was her wealth.

The question was as who among the elite would be invited.

The first to receive this so-called golden ticket was the multi-billionaire Jameson Frederick Stevens, whose income and holdings made everyone else who was not Jameson Frederick Stevens, but had money, jealous. Those who did not have that kind of money were not, of course, jealous. But that was because they could not even imagine what it might be like to be so wealthy.

There were very specific rules regarding the Cassandra Christmas as it was now rumored to be called. First, and this was especially upsetting to Jameson Frederick Stevens, the invite stipulated that he was not allowed to tell or communicate to anyone that he was given an invitation. So, to be chosen for this most prestigious experience had a price that was almost unbearable to the super wealthy. That said, Stevens assumed that after the party was over, he could reveal the truth and let his lawyers deal with the fallout.

This party was therefore then so elite and exclusive that he would not know who was going to be there. He could guess, of course. He knew those who were like him in the various categories by which he considered success to be measured.

The one thing he did know, though, was that to be on her party list this year meant that you were more than an influencer yourself, you were recognized by her.

Stevens was not known to go anywhere without his assistants or his bodyguard, let alone his lawyer (at least one of them), so he had to take certain precautions. Lying to them about where he was going would prove easier said than done. That said, he had not gotten to where he was by telling the truth.

So, he constructed a lie to cover his evening. His alibi was perfect in its non-committal nature. It was a strange crossroads map of suggestion and partial possibility that would confuse all those closest to him to at least not know the truth until at least a few days after the event.

He almost felt young again with these deceits. As if lying to those closest to him somehow showed he still had it in him.

At this point, he now trusted others to lie on his behalf. Where and when he was going would be Saturday, December 13th in Malibu, California.

He had also forgotten how much he used to enjoy driving a car. Or racing along the coast while hugging the curves and scaring tourists in their uninsured rentals.

When he arrived at Alala's secret location, he found a mansion that overlooked the coast. Surprisingly, this estate was not any mansion, beachfront or cliffside location he had been aware of. He remarked to himself, actually out loud which speaks to the enormity of it all, how amazing it must be to have the kind of money that would render one's holdings invisible to the rest of the world.

It took a lot to make him jealous. But jealous he was.

He was not surprised, of course, that there was his own personal valet waiting for him. One whose sole purpose that night was to ensure that Mr. Stevens's car was going to be taken care of.

Mr. Stevens was led in and, of course, he saw all those he expected to see. There were only twelve guests there, eleven in addition to him. He knew it would be exclusive and it was. The servants outnumbered the guests three or four to one. And that did not include those preparing the meals or serving the drinks.

There was Abner Akins, the game creator, who encouraged more children, from the ages of ten to eighty, to murder, at least digitally and online, than anyone in known history. His monies were built on killing, and a killing is what he made with every new game release. He built everything on encouraging a certain aspect of heartlessness in those who played his games.

It was often speculated that he was encouraging murder as a justifiable option in the future. Like a possibility that should be considered. If only to quell the possibility of over-population, though this doesn't even seem to be an issue anymore.

Monica D'blonsky, who made anorexia a fad to be adored and embraced, was also there, waiting for the next course of hors d'oeuvres to be served. Her mantra was that if the camera adds ten pounds, lose thirty. And this was marketed primarily to all those who liked to take selfies.

Dougie 'Dig Dog' Doug, the rapper who put a target on police everywhere, was there. With more than one bodyguard, which was against the rules, certainly, and spoke to a certain hypocrisy that no one wanted to talk about.

And there were others, including a banker who had foreclosed on more people than any banker in the history of the world. To many he was known as Mr. Homeless. That said, his tent company also seemed to do quite well as a result. And there was an actor who promoted more about her politics than was ever involved in being part of a story that ever mattered.

Jameson Frederick Stevens saw the usual suspects. He had seen them at parties before and knew that he would see them again, though trends might advocate that eventually, based on the tastes of the public, that they might not all be in this number in the years to come.

Because of Alala's heritage, all the food was from ancient Grecian recipes. From rare versions of Tzatziki to lost recipes of Souvlaki to the very best of Moussaka to even Gemista, there was nothing that was not available. If you do not know what these dishes are, do not feel bad, because they were all Greek to most in attendance as well.

Those there were there for one reason. They all wanted to meet and shake hands with Alala. She was not just an influencer, she was 'the' influencer. And all considered what their party favor might be. Real estate perhaps?

Also of note, and this was most frustrating for them all, there were no mirrors. Even in the bathrooms. In fact, as the guests began to make themselves at home and needed the restrooms, the lack of a way to look at themselves became almost infuriating. And because their smart phones were taken at the door, no one was even able to use them to look upon themselves which made the evening, for some, even more impossible. Others, of course, looked at their bottom line as a truer reflection of their worth.

They spoke to each other, of course, having the same conversations, speaking words that were rote, words told dozens of times before in just as many conversations and podcasts, talking about whatever was new. Whatever seemed like something that could be hash-tagged or forwarded. Whatever might become viral after the gala.

But, again, the point of the evening was meeting her.

Seeing her.

Alala Cassandra.

The sculptress.

The mystery.

There were drinks as well, social lubricants to ensure an evening of enjoyment. Ouzo was especially available. As was Ambrosia which spoke of the nectars of the olden gods and their curses and blessings on mankind themselves.

The guests drank and drank.

After all, there was no one to see them. Or judge them. And that was the point. That no one would see them.

Except for Alala. Alala Cassandra.

They had come for her. But she had invited them because she knew something about them that they had never dared to consider.

That the world would be a better place without them.

A kinder place.

A better one.

It was Christmas. And there was much need in the world. So much that could be done. And instead, they were here. Drinking. Eating. Celebrating their hypocrisy. Reveling in the lie and the deceit that was their lives. That who they were mattered to all others.

When Alala finally revealed herself. Her words were simple.

She simply said that this was a time in which we should not look at ourselves, but to others. And then encouraged them to look at her.

It was then that she finally showed her face.

But it wasn't just about her face, which looked both terribly old in the eyes, but was unwrinkled and unlined when it came to her skin.

It was also about her hair. Not the locks, the length or the color but something else entirely.

Her hair was made of snakes.

Whether you would call her a Medusa or a Gorgon it matters not. The point is that to look upon her was to become instantly frozen in a state that could only be called being turned to stone.

She was far older than anyone had even considered.

If there was a cure for the twelve statues that remained, and those of the bodyguards that came with the rapper, that is unknown.

There are some that suggest that the stones might cry out or even be moved by a word, but that is not the point of this story. It's not one of redemption even if this is Christmas.

This is the story of bad people. Bad people who got their comeuppance at Christmas. There is certainly grace for all, but even that kindness runs out one day.

Like the sands of time.

Like the last grains that fall through an hourglass.

Sand, to be fair to sand, was once not sand.

Sand was once stone. Stone that was worn down, broken down and granularized by time. And whatever it was, was forgotten, like the name Jameson Frederick Stevens would one day be.

What is equally important to note, though, was that the statues of the twelve in attendance were donated to certain auctions which raised a modest amount of funds for the hungry and the homeless. And these usually sold to the estates of the twelve who had gone missing and were never heard from again.

Those statues, though, later, after certain estates fell from power and influence, would be put on auction to be bid upon once again years later, but would sell for a far lesser amount.

And even then, not all of them sold. That said, and for their sake, with all desire to show kindness, maybe their features, now cast in stone, lasted longer than those of flesh and blood.

If you are one, like the guests at the party, to think such a thing matters.

 Already Wrapped

There is a legend in ancient Egypt that a slave once collected from the gods themselves, a bag of dust that had been shaken from their very feet. They say the slave dared to love a Princess of the Nile and planned to give her the dust in hopes that she would never age and remain beautiful for all time. When news of this eternal sand of timelessness reached the Pharaoh, the bag, its contents, and the slave were ordered before the king.

The Pharaoh was dying and hoped that the bag's contents would save him. The slave, of course, hid the dust from the bag and replaced it with ordinary sand. The bag of false dust was immediately seized for the Pharaoh's use. But when the King of Egypt died, the slave's ruse was uncovered, and he was imprisoned. Even then, the slave refused to reveal where he had hidden the timeless dust and was ceremonially executed and mummified. His soul was to sleep until the day the Pharaoh returned from the dead to punish the slave further.

Three jeweled beetles were placed on the slave's casket to make certain that no one would break the seal and awaken him. The jewels were thought to have dark mystical powers, as well as the power to bind and the power to imprison. And as long as they were near the slave, he would remain in the bondage of the Pharaoh. That was thousands of years ago.

The three jeweled Beetles were the first things the archeologists found. The Beetles were flown immediately to England. The Mummy was sent a day later.

So, the fact that a Mummy walked the streets of London that Christmas Eve should come as no surprise to those that know the legend.

Teenagers thought it was a movie stunt and laughed and honked the horns of their cars when they passed.

One woman thought it was someone who had been in a terrible accident. She stuffed a few coins in the Mummy's bandages and told it that she hoped he'd have a better year next year.

A few over-zealous religious followers insisted it was a "swaddling clothes" celebration. They proceeded to go home to mummify themselves. They also called their friends. After a little while, there were now maybe fifty or so more people dressed as mummies walking the streets of London.

The British are very famous for their fashion statements and for the fads and the almost cult-like trends that begin in their land. But this, this was strange even for England.

The Mummy that had been a slave, though, had no statement to make, apart from the desire to love. And this is the plight of many on Christmas.

There is no place to go, really. And home, if there is a home, even that may not feel like home. And so, you wander. And you hope that you will find something of significance that night. Even somewhere to stay when so many doors seem closed.

Now, the museum discovered that one of their Mummies was missing. Those they found walking the streets did not act like Mummies at all. Ironically, they tried to convince the curators of the museum to rethink their eternal destinies.

The real Mummy continued to wander into the night.

Now there is something to realize about most stories about mummies, and that is they are stories about a love that transcends death and generations and time. The process of becoming a mummy is terrible and leaves the mummy far less than they were in this life. All one's vital organs are removed in the process.

So, a mummy brought back to life must move on without the guts to face the reality of their situation, and without the heart to see that this love that they seek is to someone that cannot love them back. Someone who has moved on without them. There is always something blocking their way. And perhaps this is the basis of all the lonely Christmases for those who wished to have someone to share it with.

In the case of this slave, there was an extra curse, and it was the fact that she was a princess and he was only a slave. And there is nothing worse for a person than wanting to love and not being able to.

That said, the Mummy was very surprised to see her, yes Her, working in a video store. He did not know what a video was, but he did not care. He was actually very fortunate she did work in a video store because few other retail operations are open that late, especially on Christmas Eve.

She was there. He peered through the window, and there she was. She wasn't dressed like a daughter of the Nile. But it was her, here, now. He had no doubts. It had been a long time. And his memories were not everything they once were, but it had to be her.

He entered the video store and dragged himself up to the counter.

She looked at him.

"Yeah?" she asked.

He began to breathe heavily which in itself was a surprise because he had no lungs either.

She got nervous and grabbed the phone to call the police. He did not know what she was doing but was convinced that she did not recognize him as he had her.

"It is I, Princess," said the Mummy through the material.

"What did you call me?"

"Princess."

She smirked. "And you are?"

"Your servant? Don't you recognize me?"

"Not through the bandages. Are you…?"

"Oh. I am so sorry. The gods take me for a fool. We must

be careful. Your father's spies are everywhere. I had to see you again, you understand. I had to. It was worth it all for this moment."

"So, you're my servant?" she asked, playing along.

"Yes. Now you see. You do. You do recognize me."

"Oh, sure I do," she said with mock recognition.

"It's an amazing thing. The gift I was bringing you, the dust of the gods, I had entrusted it to another servant when I was caught. But instead of getting it to you, he put the dust in my wrappings. It saved me."

The Mummy began to pull the bandages from his head, unwinding them as quickly as he could. The bandages, and the dust that was in them, and even some insect skeletons fell to the ground.

"Can you do that somewhere else? I'm going to have to clean up your mess now."

"You would have to clean up?" The Mummy, dumbstruck, continued to unwrap himself.

But where any museum curator would have expected the husk of a man, shriveled beyond recognition underneath, no such vision awaited the video store worker. She saw before her a handsome young man, a little dirty, but beautiful in every respect.

"Not bad." She smiled to herself. "You're my servant, you say?"

"You would clean up after me, a slave?"

The Mummy was mystified by the notion of the princess cleaning. Perhaps she was no longer a princess. If she was a slave now too, there was nothing to keep them apart. This was wonderful.

The video store worker was entranced, so much so that she ignored every warning and piece of advice she ever heard about what to do if someone completely dressed in gauze and dirt came up to you and called you Princess.

"Hey. I have to close up here in a few minutes. You want to get some coffee?"

"What is coffee?"

"You know, it's what you drink to keep from having to sleep. It's what you drink when you have to wake up."

"I have slept a very long to time to see you again. I would not like to again."

"Then coffee's just the thing… again? Never mind. Tell me about it later."

And he did. He told her about the Nile and about their love and about how long he has been waiting for her.

At first he was deeply hurt by the fact that she could not remember him, and then realized that like himself, she too was probably cursed to forget him. Perhaps the Pharaoh's chief priests had blinded her to love.

So he continued. He told her about the dust shaken from the feet of the gods. He told her about how her father wanted the dust for himself. And he told her how he hid it but did not know what would be done to him. He told her how amazed he was to see that she is here, now, and never needed the eternal sand at all.

Now this girl, whose name was Kara and who actually was partly Egyptian by blood, listened intently. He had awakened something in her. Something so deep and so profound that she could not speak, and hardly dared to breathe.

He had awakened something in her. Oh, she knew she was no princess, but somehow, she felt like one in his presence.

To have someone love you so, since well before you were born, even if it was just a story, someone so perfect that they would wait thousands of years to just see you. Who wouldn't want to believe that?

"So this is love," she said.

Of course, he was thinking the same thing as he looked at her.

Fully restored and more so.

There was a new heart where the old one had been taken. And the guts to hope for a better day regardless of the ones that had come before it.

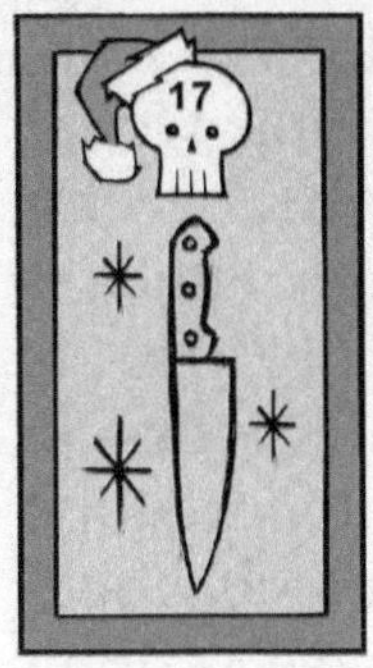

And to All a Good Knife

We all have purposes. A reason to be. It's that thing that makes us, you know.

What we're here for. But sometimes… sometimes…

I didn't want to be a knife, not anymore.

Actually, I'm not sure I ever wanted to be a knife at all. But certainly, I didn't want to be a knife anymore.

I was not a chef's knife like I might have wanted to be, dealing with rare cuts of beef and vegetables hand-selected by someone in a tall white hat who wanted to bring art to the tastebuds of the hungry. I wasn't a knife used by young lovers to carve initials and promises into the side of a tree. Or a knife ready to open letters from friends or Christmas cards. I wasn't even a throwing knife who might have enjoyed traveling as a part of a circus.

No.

I was a serial murderer's knife.

A killer's knife.

I was the instrument by which my holder would kill his victims.

There is also no such thing as a truly clean knife when you're my kind of knife. No matter the washing or the sharpening, we are never truly clean. There's always something left behind. Maybe that's part of why so many of the murdered become ghosts and haunt serial killers and, well, one- or two-time killers alike. I wonder what the threshold number of kills is to make one a serial killer.

Not being able to talk back, I don't think I'll ever learn because serial killers aren't that self-aware. But you would think that they would be. Especially because serial killers talk a lot. My holder has something called Tinnitus, which is a ringing in his ears. Maybe his constant talking was just to drown it out. But from what I hear, most serial killers talk to themselves all the time and they don't pay a lot of attention to the objects in the room, those that might still absorb words and sounds even if the killer assumed that those objects don't really hear them.

Like me.

And so I heard my share about the architecture of a death and what makes a really good kill. How much preparation goes into this sort of thing and how there is a process that takes the primal desire, as they would call a primal need, to kill. How the weather plays a part and how many outdoor kills are determined by whether or not it is raining or it looks like it is about to, which makes me think that many a meteorologist is an accomplice without ever even knowing.

Then there was how to target an individual. How to follow them and learn their habits and their routines. Who is important to them and who, potentially, in their life, might be potentially a hero and try to bring the killer to justice.

My holder also repeated himself. So much so that if his victims were privy and listened, they might welcome death just to not have to hear this guy anymore.

Eventually, even for someone like me, a killer's monologue becomes quite tedious. And quite dull no matter how often I may be sharpened in the process.

I had had my fill about all the ins and outs of a perfect stabbing and kill, and why some deserved to die while others were allowed to live.

And no matter how many times I was used to ending a life for the sake of my holder's art, it still made me sick inside, like up to my hilt, to be a part of this.

I was a knife and I was being misused even if I was still being used to cut, which is, of course, our ultimate purpose.

I was forged. I was tested. Even though my holder was not. I knew I was meant for something better though my holder, the killer, clearly, did not believe there was even such a thing as a higher purpose of being.

Which brings me to those days before Christmas. Because of the monotony of this life that I had become accustomed to, I didn't take a lot of notice of the days of the week or the weeks of the month or even the months of the year.

The cold, though, that… that I noticed.

As opposed to the brutality I was used to, there's a 'brutality' to the coming of cold weather. The colder, the more brittle for something like me. The colder, the less smooth the cut. Which is why he would keep me in his pocket and away from the elements in the colder parts of the year. But there are also many types of cold, including the temperature of a human heart. Cold is cold.

And so it was that, that one year my holder decided that he wanted me to help him kill a street-corner Santa Claus. And Christmas was coming.

Maybe it was the fact that come this time of year, he kept on ringing his bell. And everyone cheered for a ringing that was in his ears all the time. Or maybe it was because of the costume or even the idea of Santa as a concept. Or maybe it was because he knew that Santa was a judge and he refused to be judged by anyone because he considered himself to be such an artist. Regardless, there was a target on this Santa, this Santa-wannabe or Santa-paid-to-be regardless of the situation.

And this target meant that he would not get to ring-a-ding-ding this Christmas, let alone the New Year.

If some would ask for who the bell tolls, well, it would toll for Santa in the very near future.

My holder prepared for that night he would approach his next victim, or canvas, as he considered them.

But, as always, he didn't consider that he was wrong. Or that most deserve to live.

The Santa in question struggled with something called carpal tunnel syndrome. This meant his wrist was terribly sore and made ringing a bell for so many hours a day a terrible sadness. But he felt good about the work he was doing for others and was now headed home. It was walkable. A bus would have been better in this city, but it was walkable. And so, he walked because he wanted to see the rest of the world. He wanted to see all those he might have begged from and maybe some of the people he might actually have helped, though he never knew them personally. And he wanted to see beyond his ringing, into their world. Into their realities. And maybe, even to not resent those that never gave, by seeing them as people.

It didn't take long for my holder to catch up to this Santa, who was still dressed like Santa. This meant that there were times that children would stop him in hopes of telling him what they want for Christmas or the half-inebriated already would offer to buy him a drink. So it always took him a while to get home.

So catch up to him my holder did.

He wasn't even ringing the bell.

Which made no difference to my holder at all.

My hilt was grabbed, and I was pulled from the darkness of a pocket and thrust into another darkness altogether.

The man playing Santa was used to pain, but not like this.

I was pulled out and readied to make another stab.

I was now covered in Santa's blood.

My holder almost never did anything when it was possible for someone else to see. And there was new snow on the ground which meant it might be easier to follow a trail… or that trail might be covered up all the quicker.

The holder used me again and the victim fell to the ground. But this was a Santa, which meant there was good will, whether deserved or not, that most would offer up. And on a busy street on the holidays, it's almost never possible to do anything in secret.

Santa screamed from the sidewalk. And the scream was heard and heard by more than one.

My holder, maybe overwhelmed and therefore sloppy by the ringing in his own ears and not those of this would-pretendto-be Santa, ran off, and for the first time, I was left behind.

I was there, in the dark. Abandoned. Blood was now running from me, onto the pavement. I could be seen.

A crowd gathered around us. Me and Santa. They stared down at the man and were deeply concerned. Some said prayers, and others cursed the city. This was Santa and he was bleeding into the gutter, the snow around him reddening.

But there was one, one that stopped, and stooped, and told the others to step away, just a little, so he could work.

He told them he was a doctor.

He took hold of me.

And I was no longer the knife I had been.

I was no longer a tool used to kill, but what, in his hand, might be used to heal.

I was now a scalpel.

He went to work in the worst of conditions. In the dark. In the cold. On the hardest and smelliest and probably most bacteria-covered concrete in the world. But it didn't stop him from working. Some of the onlookers took out their phones to offer some light.

He saved the life of this would-be Santa. And he used me to do it.

And that's how this doctor saved my life too. It was a miracle.

Maybe that's what Christmas is, maybe that's what it means, that the miracle isn't just for one. But for many.

And yes, the killer got away to kill another day. At least until someone stopped him.

I guess that's what ghosts are here for.

Have Yourself a Rosemary Little Christmas

I know I'm not supposed to feel self-conscious about my weight anymore. I know that the world has changed its opinion on so-called curves and rolls and there is now room for differences in size and stature. That there is no better and there is no worse and everyone needs to be accepted for who and what they are. Every volume is welcome. Even mine. Even me.

But then there's the health aspect of it all. And there is airline travel and having to buy two seats and, well, then I think about my own lifespan, and I… need to do something because this isn't healthy.

So…

My name is Steve.

Steve. Stephan. Steven. No matter what I get called, I still need to lose weight. I'm a fatty. In California terms, fat is like five pounds. Not in my case. But I am in California and no matter where I go, people look at me like I'm smoking cigarettes or something.

So, I decided to seek out a way to lose weight and embraced a diet. I sought out specialists. I searched for the unique. And embraced a little bit of the bonkers because other diets didn't work for me. Neither did pills. The problem was that most of the diets I was introduced to, well, they really weren't for me. And so, I had to keep on searching.

And finally, I found someone who promised me that there would be nothing left of the old me once my diet was done.

His name was Doctor Franklin Austice and what was missing from my diet was rosemary. Consuming as much of it as I could would make a giant difference and even get me an invitation to a very special dinner in Carmel in the old James House.

How could I say no?

The price was right. And I wouldn't have to pinch pennies. Or my tummy. In fact, it was almost like one of those diet experiments where they pay you to try to find a cure for something. I could eat what I wanted as long as I chewed a sprig of Rosemary while I did it. It was hardly a loss, and most things, including certain desserts were better on this diet. Who would have thought a rhubarb shortcake would be even better with rosemary? I almost regretted trying to lose weight considering this discovery. Okay, maybe I did regret it a bit.

Thirty days and I didn't lose a pound. In fact, I gained. Almost five pounds. My dietician said it was perfectly natural and eventually I would lose weight, but I couldn't help thinking about Rosemary's Baby, for obvious reasons this being a rosemary diet and all, and how she lost weight when she was pregnant with Satan's baby and the doctor there said that eventually she would gain.

My friends also didn't believe in the diet. They kept asking about the doctor and who he was. But I reminded them that this was California, the home of so many diets, so many health fads, so many celebrities ways-to-lose and so many Ojai hippie-like agendas for losing weight that who was to say. They didn't argue with me, but also, no one really likes to argue with anyone here. It's just not accepting. Kind of like how there are Sizzler steak houses here even though they were all closed in every other state. Or why I can still get Mojo potatoes and the all-you-eat pizza buffet at a Shakey's pizza. They say that if you can make it in New York, you can make it anywhere. I like to think of California as the place where if you couldn't make it anywhere else, you can still make it here.

So again, saying nay to the nay-sayers, the Rosemary diet was what I was on right now and it was taking me to an amazing party in a house fashioned after King Arthur's birthplace. I didn't do the diet as well as I should have, but it's the holidays and everybody cheats on their diet a little. It's almost a law, and if it isn't, it certainly is a rule or at least a guideline.

When I got to the party, everyone looked at me. But it wasn't in a bad way. At least I didn't think so. I wore a sprig of Rosemary pinned to my lapel like I was told. And it was quite the conversation starter.

There was wine, of course, a certain Barbera which I learned came from Italy and was not that common. But they all said it would pair well. Something about the plum, the lavender, and the oak of it all embracing the savory meat that was adorned with rosemary.

By this point, I was a little tired of rosemary and thought I might look forward to one of the other dishes.

It was then that I began to realize that there were certain guests at this soiree that were like me. There was another guest, roughly my size, that seemed to have a crown of basil around his head like he was adorned in the day of Socrates. He was being served, as well as those who seemed to show him special attention, a Sauvignon Blanc with, what I overheard, a special acidity that would be perfect. And then there was a rather stout woman whose name was Darla but was more of a Meg (as in Nutmeg) based on how she smelled. She was being served a Pinot Noir from New Zealand. Some of the guests that were not sprigged or garnished were encouraging Meg to get close to the basil guy, suggesting that nutmeg and basil always go well together.

I didn't like the way the guests were looking at us. And began really regretting that new extra weight as well.

The chefs were cheered when they entered. And they all seemed to beckon the applause to be turned in our direction.

I was taken to another room with Darla (Nutmeg) and the Basil guy whose name I learned was Johnny. And there were two others. The woman smelled of lemon and the other had a whiskey smell about him. And not from his breath. Clearly he enjoyed his diet. I see him as a Four Roses small batch guy. But an awful lot of that small batch.

I was quick, at least in realizing what was happening. I started backing away from the others. Which meant they were the first to see, what I can only assume were the butchers for this evening's meal.

This was like some kind of Hotel California mentality, I thought. Hannibal Lector had nothing on these guys, except, of course, that everyone knew about him and this was being done in secret.

Lots of people go missing in California. I never imagined that this was how it was for some of them. Homeless problem, my butt. Speaking of which, I didn't like how they were looking at mine at that moment and had visions of a rosemary rump roast, slightly salted. Or assaulted in my case.

They were cannibals and we were the main dishes.

So I ran. I ran as if my life depended on it, which it probably always did. So at least there's that. And I've been running ever since.

I sometimes remember back to that particular Christmas. It wasn't the feast of Steven, no matter what King Wenceslas says in the song. But it was of Johnny, Darla, Todd and Janice.

The Sock Monster

I'm not sure when I became a damned thing. Or, perhaps, for the younger readers, a darned thing.

I'm a sock. And I've had three lives. Most socks only have one. And that is to be a sock. To cover a foot and to step into that middle space of allowing a foot to join a shoe with a little more comfort. In this role, we also are asked to absorb certain smells from the foot so as to not make the shoe unbearable to wear for as long as possible. In this life, we are washed often. Dried often. And we are the first, well before feet or shoes, to show the signs of age. Of being worn out.

Either we are worn out or we lose our match, the other sock, which would go with the other shoe and the other foot. If one of us shows signs of wear before the other, usually in the form of a hole, chances are both of us socks are rendered useless. And tossed out.

There's not a lot of glamor to this life. And it doesn't last long. But sometimes, there is a second life to socks, a second opportunity to fit or fill a need.

And that is what I became.

I became a sock monster.

Perhaps it began when the other me was lost. But regardless, there were other things that were lost as well that added to my transformation and to my second life. There were buttons from a torn shirt that became my new eyes.

Was I afraid? No. Frayed yes. Afraid no. Where before I was filled by a foot, now I would be filled by a hand.

And then there was some material that was a zigzag design inspired by a tile floor from a famous television series that became my mouth. You would think that eyes and a mouth would be enough. That technically the use of a hand inside me would be enough to suggest a mouth.

Other lost things were sewed into me, all were intended to cause fear and suggest the evil puppet I was becoming.

My smell, for all those who smelt me, was terrible. Where socks are washed, sock puppets are not. Like never. Perhaps it's in fear of the button eyes being lost in the wash, or maybe it's just the sense that there is nothing to be cleaned. That the dirtier the monster the better. Regardless, the smells of a certain left foot and an even certainer left sneaker remained.

I was made into a monster and monsters are not meant to smell good.

Yes, I was a monster now. But to be fair, I was no more a monster than the hand and the arm and the body I was an extension of. The boy, in and of himself, was also especially a monster.

It's not that he was particularly evil. Only that he was a boy. And that he was a brother. And this was enough to torment his sister.

And so he would go at it. One day he grabbed her doll with me. Another day, he toppled her tea party. And still another he rubbed me all over her toothbrush telling her that I could only improve her breath. This was a lie, of course, as I knew of no monsters, including myself, who had such breath-redeeming power. And if we did, would it even be right to call me a monster?

And there was still the smell.

Here's also the thing about monsters. Eventually we stop being scary. We lose our ability to surprise and disgust.

And I was at that point. He chased her with me over and over again. More than once, she came into her room and I was hanging, as if hung, from the chain that turned her light and ceiling fan on. Sometimes she opened a drawer and I was there. Other times I was on his hand and he would attack, always hoping for a scream, always reminding me that I only had a life to make her scream and he could throw me away any time he wanted. Anytime I ever stopped from scaring her. And therefore, pleasing him.

Her screams pleased her brother to no end. On another occasion, she tried to put her foot, already socked, into a shoe, only to find I was already there.

And it continued.

She played the oboe. But quit when she opened the tiny case and found me wrapped around and covering her oboe mouthpiece. I think that even one of my buttons bent one of the arms on the instrument. Her Mom yelled at her brother a lot over that one. I think it had to do with the idea of the mouthpiece and the bent arm, but I was bored, and it was just screaming at that point. And some crying. Maybe even more crying than screaming.

Anyhow, there's only so long that I would be able to scare her. And so, one terrible Christmas eve, when my scare didn't make a bit of difference, I was dropped and abandoned and left with nothing on the floor, close enough to the Christmas tree.

And there I sat. There I lay, like a dead thing. Like the abandoned monster I was. No longer scary, smelling worse than ever. Abandoned. There was no right for me to exist anymore. I was left.

Left alone. Just like I was always told I would be. There was a fire in the fireplace between me and the tree. Being consumed for Christmas. That's where I was.

The fire seemed to reach out to me. More than the glimmer of blinking lights on the tree. And though I knew it would be more than likely that I would not burn, but instead be thrown in a dumpster, that didn't mean that I wouldn't be burned eventually or perhaps be buried forever with so much other trash that had lost its purpose in the world.

This was what I was.

An empty thing.

Made uglier by time. And the whims and selfishness of children.

And maybe that was the reason he picked me up. And by him, I mean Santa. He had come. I'm not exactly sure how he got through the fire to get to the tree and to bring presents. The fire continued, no longer roaring, but it clearly wasn't doused by the coming of snow-covered boots. I could still feel its warmth. And even that was surprising because we socks are used to bringing warmth and not usually experiencing it. It would take a while to realize that the warmth was not coming from the fire but from Santa himself. How could someone from the North Pole bring this? Warmth of all things.

He picked me up, very carefully.

He looked into my eyes, holding me from the toe part of myself. He wasn't scared, he didn't jump. There was a sadness to him, but a joy as well. As if looking upon the world's children had brought a poignancy and an understanding that equaled complete compassion. He clearly knew pain. I didn't expect that or was even capable of understanding just how deep his eyes saw. I only had buttons after all.

And then he began to speak.

"I'm sorry, my friend. I'm sorry you have been dealt with so much cruelty. I'm sorry for your scars, which in your case are holes that need only to be mended. I'm sorry you were used to frighten others. I'm sorry that when you were used in this second life of yours, it was used only to frighten."

He continued.

"There is a third life waiting for you, and that's what I mean for you to have this evening. And tomorrow morning. And perhaps all the Christmas mornings to come. Maybe there is a fourth life for you, even after this, though I am not sure if socks have souls. Shoes do. But socks, I don't know, for there are some mysteries hidden even to me."

He took the buttons off me, but I could see better than ever before. Where there were holes, there were not holes any more. Where there were zigzagged add-ons to make me look angry, those zigzags took on an ornate beauty as if all I had experienced had earned this, though this was also in itself a gift.

I was not a monster anymore. I knew that. But I also wasn't

sure what I had become. Santa spoke more. But his words were a mystery to me. He spoke of me needing to accept that sometimes I would be full but sometimes I would be empty, but never truly empty because of Christmas.

He no longer held me by my toe area. He now held me by the other end and he apologized for the pain I was about to feel. All the holes in me were mended, were made and sewed and looked like there wasn't a hole at all. But a new hole was made. It went through one side of me and then the other. He apologized for the pain of course.

"The nail is necessary, I'm afraid. As are the holes. For these are the holes and the wounds of love."

He hung me above the fire, and not by the toe. And then began to fill me with all manner of gifts. Of fruits and candies. Of toys and playthings. I had never felt so full in my life. So warm. And for the first time, I was not afraid of when, the next morning, I would be empty again.

"Christmas changes the world for all of us. It turns the world upside down. It did long ago and does so still. And will do so forever. Long after the likes of us. You were never the monster, only the brother was, and sometimes brothers take a while to stop being so."

He left a little after that and I hung there, until the next morning, where I became a gift and not a torment to a certain little girl. One who didn't even recognize me.

I don't know about the rest of the world, but this Christmas did turn my world upside down. And it made me free. To be filled. To be emptied. And filled again next Christmas.

Free. No longer a puppet. Free. No longer afraid.

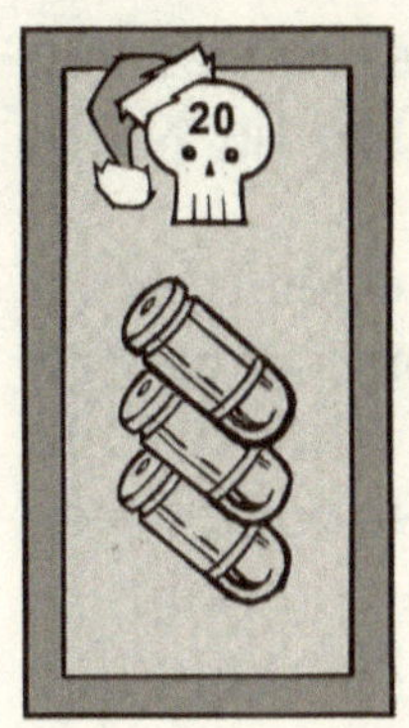

The December Man

The December Man entered town around the time it began to snow. He didn't ride in. He had no horse. If he had had one, the last year had taken care of that. So, he walked. His work was almost done. He smiled to himself knowing there was indeed some good he had accomplished. Christmas had put the year before it in perspective. And regrets made no difference now. Not on New Year's Eve. He had a few hours left at best. And he knew it was almost over. For this man, this killer in the eyes of so many was about to die.

He would not die by hanging, or by being shot, or by the hands of other men. Although mortality was measured largely by the gun and the trigger and an ill manner at this time in history, such a death was not meant for a December Man. Disease was also a fitful equalizer, but not for one like him.

To be fair, he was tired. And death was not something he was choosing for himself. If it were up to him, he'd have continued on the way he had, for good or bad.

Some wanted him dead. And not only dead, but forgotten, as if he had never been at all. He had brought them nothing but sadness and loss.

But for others, there was something almost sad mixed with his coming death. But they too were happy to see him go. As it was with all that like him that had come before.

The snow was falling harder now. And most of those that

lived in town, had either returned to their homes to wait out the storm with their families, or had collected in the North Star Saloon for the warmth each other could bring.

And in the jail, on the end of town, Deputy Chester Tyler sat alone, thinking about the future and thinking about not being a part of it. Chester put a single bullet into his gun. It was a Colt. And without going into too much of Chester's past, what needs to be known is that Chester did not want to live any more.

But he was also afraid to die. He took the bullet out of the colt again and took a drink from the bottle in a drawer in his desk. The bottle was half-empty. That was quick.

The town had almost no crime, not since the Sheriff had faced the John Miller gang and introduced the notion of a citizen's rights as more than just a chance dream. The Sheriff changed this city almost a year before. And with the help of his deputy, brought twelve evil men to justice and brought justice back to the town.

Chester put the bullet back in the gun.

They say 'with the help of his deputy' because that's how the Sheriff put it. What they should really say is that the Sheriff took on all twelve outlaws on his own. And his deputy cowered beneath a cot in one of the jail cells. They should really talk about the coward that he was. But that wasn't the Sheriff's way.

Chester took the bullet out of the gun. He looked at it. And put it in again. He took it out a second later. The process of loading and unloading continued well into the night and well into the bottle of whiskey.

Chester thought to himself how it's not what people know about you that makes it hard to live with them, it's what they don't know about you that makes it impossible. He was a coward when the town needed him most. And when he pulled himself from his cot, and saw that the city was saved, he didn't feel any better. He felt worse. The city had been saved, the John Miller gang was wiped out, and it was all done without him.

Chester looked across the desk. Where'd that bullet go? He rummaged like a fearful man who'd lost his riches only to find the bullet was already in the gun. He unloaded the gun. And looked at the bullet.

Chester wondered how many lies the Sheriff would tell about him this time. Would he say that Chester cared too much? Would he say that Chester couldn't live with having killed even bad men for the cause of good people? Would the town cry on his behalf? Would they wail for him? Would the daughters of this town grieve the loss of a possible suitor? Chester did not know. And was, in all honesty, a little afraid to even consider the possibility.

Chester would smoke a cigarette and then smoke himself. That was the plan.

A plan that changed the moment the December Man entered the jail.

Chester was, obviously, upset by this stranger and his interruption.

"We're closed," he spouted, putting his hat over his gun.

"Not to me." The December Man nodded, sitting down across from Chester. The December man looked at the hat, then at Chester.

Chester looked at the hat, then the desk and had a terrible thought. Was the gun loaded? He looked for the bullet and saw nothing. Was it too under that hat?

"What do you want?" said Chester, trying to draw attention away from the hat.

"I'm a killer. I want you to take me into custody."

Chester sat up at this. "Who'd you kill?"

"Do you know the John Miller gang?"

Chester found he could hardly breathe. There was something clearly wrong with this man. "Are… you saying you killed the John Miller gang?"

The stranger just sat there and took another glance at the hat.

Chester didn't even think about the gun under the hat. He had forgotten about the bullet as well.

"The Sheriff brought the John Miller gang to justice, Mister. It wasn't you."

"No. It wasn't you," the stranger said with a smile. The stranger knew. He knew Chester was a coward. But that was impossible. Did the Sheriff tell someone?

Chester wondered what was happening. His reason was beginning to run wild.

"Was the John Miller gang all you… I mean, did you kill anyone other than them?"

"Oh yes."

"How many?"

"Millions."

Chester was almost in shock when the stranger reached forward tossing the hat to the side and picked up the Colt. He aimed it at Chester in almost the same move.

The stranger looked at Chester, now with a knowing sadness. "Death is romantic until we stop courting it and are forced to take the vow, isn't it, Deputy?"

"Who are you?"

"I am the December Man. And you want to die. Since that is all that I am ever credited with, I thought I'd help you."

Chester looked at the gun and had to admit that he did not want to die. That's why he hid in the first place.

"I don't want to die," he said.

"But wasn't this gun loaded for that purpose?"

"Yes, but…" Chester wondered for a moment if the gun was loaded. The stranger knew so much, though.

"Wouldn't it be easier if I did this for you, if I pulled the trigger? The Sheriff could tell everyone in town that an outlaw broke in and killed you? I'm your friend, Chester."

"But…"

"What time is it?"

Chester opened his pocket watch. "Almost midnight."

"Well come on Chester, I don't have all night. What's it going to be?"

"Did you really kill over a million people? I mean, if you did, there'd have to be a pretty big reward on your head."

"I am to blame for every death. Every murder is attributed to me." The December Man spoke these words with a notable heaviness. This wasn't pride speaking. It was something deeper, something somber.

"What are you?"

"I am like you, a nobody, a number."

"What is your number?"

"1869," said the December Man.

"That's the year."

"Yes. The January child will soon be born. But there is one more life to claim."

"Are you talking about me?" asked Chester.

"Life is given and forgotten. Death, though, that is never forgotten. Do you know how many more people were born this year than died?"

"No."

The stranger pointed the gun at Chester. "That's the point. Whether this gun is empty or it's loaded is immaterial to me. You, though, you can live or you can die. It's up to you."

Chester sat, unsure of all. And then he lunged at the stranger, the self-proclaimed December Man. Chester's hand gripped the end of the gun like a drowning man would a piece of wood. The two men struggled and fell to the floor.

Chester pulled the gun from the stranger's hands and pointed it at the December Man. It was not the sound of a gunshot that was heard when the trigger was pulled. It was the ringing of the New Year. It was the stroke of Midnight.

Chester left the body of the December Man on the floor. He turned back to the table. It was quite by accident that he lifted his hat. He was not wondering about the bullet at all. After all, he'd pulled the trigger. The December Man was dead. But pick up his hat he did, and there under the hat, was the bullet.

Then what killed the December Man?

He turned back to the body.

But the corpse was gone, as if he had never been there at all.

Chester rubbed his eyes and took a drink.

He noticed with a smile that the bottle was still half full. Which was good, in fact, because he still had the New Year to celebrate.

As do we all.

I'll Be There in Spirit

The scarf was tight. Not like the way a mother would tie it. Or a well-meaning teacher. No. It was tight. Too tight. So tight that he could hardly breathe.

He couldn't breathe, not at all. He was about to die, strangled on his way to a Christmas party of his fellow fashion designers. He wasn't going to make it. To the party. Or in the way they talk about a dying person pulling through. He wasn't going to make it.

He had a thought as he breathed his last, which was no breath at all. First, he noticed that the scarf he was being strangled with on this terrible freezing night lacked style. And on any given day, he wouldn't be caught dead in a thing like this.

Any other given day. Not this one.

There is much to the mystery of life and death and then the afterlife. But this is about the mystery of his death. And who was responsible.

He had an amazing name. His name was Danny Rolex. And while he certainly wished that he came from the Rolex family, he did not. But growing up with a name like that was enough to push him in the direction of fashion design.

The first thing to know about our new ghost is that when he was living, people tended to say he had a big head in that way that didn't suggest a malformation but instead spoke to his pride and delusions in regard to his accomplishments and self-importance.

To be fair, though, in any creative endeavor, some self-delusion is important because there is no limit to the amount of criticism that a new creative will face in whatever industry he or she may find themselves in. A healthy denial of the truth of one's abilities is amazingly important to the process of growth as an artist.

Still, and this goes well beyond his abilities, Danny Rolex was not well liked. One rarely does the facial math to realize that having a big head often means having a big mouth. As well as other features. Maybe one's large nose in this case is easier to notice as one will often cut it off to spite oneself. Ironically for the big-headed, one's ears are rarely that large and that is always evident because of how little a big-headed person will listen to others.

Danny Rolex didn't know how the others at the party felt about him. He was about to. And one amazing thing about new ghosts, is that they really do have amazing ears. Maybe that's the problem. Because ghosts are haunted too, and it is often the delusions of their past life that haunt them.

When he arrived at the party, he waited outside for quite a while. This was because he kept putting his ghost finger up to the doorbell and naturally assumed he was pressing it. His astral finger, of course, kept going through the button which was irritating. There was a little electrical spark every time he did which didn't help him not believe it wasn't working. But that's more of an electro-plasmic, as opposed to ectoplasmic, reaction as it is.

He had remembered how cold it was before… and was grateful that he could not feel this cold anymore. But the waiting was hard for him until he realized what was going on with the doorbell. He wasn't pressing it. He couldn't press it.

This would have been quite depressing if he didn't realize a couple moments later that this also meant that he could just walk through the door.

The steps up to the party took a bit of an effort as well, not that breathing heavy or even breathing at all was really an issue for him anymore. But his feet kept moving through steps as he tried to climb them. He would move forward into the wooden stairway but not up it. And once he was completely surrounded by the wood, he would have to back up and out of the stairwell again.

This was infuriating and Danny was never known for his patience. But he also knew that if he didn't figure this out, he would never get to the party at all.

And so, very slowly, he tried to walk the steps. His steps needed to be light, as if it was more about balance than weight dispersant, not that even weight was a matter to govern him anymore. But it was like a mindset, an approach to movement that allowed him to eventually make his way up to the party.

The party, though, was not as expected. No one spoke, and while some sipped from their drinks, there was a stunned silence.

They all looked at each other in shock as if they had been given news that they could not believe.

Danny Rolex was dead. It was on the news.

And then something happened that would haunt Danny from that moment on. It would haunt him for as long as he would be a ghost. Math was never one of his specialties and would be impossible for him to calculate such a number. But regardless, something was said that he would never forget.

One of the party goers looked at the others and asked a very simple question.

"So, which of us did it?"

They all looked at each other. The silence was more silent than before. There was a slight chuckle from… somewhere. And then the entire room erupted in laughter.

Now those who make their living in the fashion industry are a very sensitive people, so it might not be fair to judge them too harshly regarding this moment. That said, in certain schools, in certain places, fashion students can be monsters and tyrants to each other more than to anyone else.

The ghost of Danny Rolex was stunned. They were all laughing. It was then that several people went to a table filled with different bottles of alcohol, including Campari, which is never a good sign if the proper amount of Gin, Sweet

Vermouth and a large ice cube is not also an accompaniment. But Negronis aside, this party was a cocktail too bitter for Danny to drink.

Who could have guessed that the death of the party had turned into the life of the party.

The fashion students drank and roared and told Danny Rolex stories that suggested that Danny's treatment of each of them was so terrible that Danny wondered if it was actually someone else they were talking about.

They hated him. They really hated him.

It could have been any of them, is what he thought. They all had their reasons for not liking him. Or perhaps they were all in on it. Maybe they drew straws to see which of them would do it. No, probably not. Joking about which of them did it would not have been the case if this were true.

So who did it?

And should he even bother? After all, if they were all this terrible, maybe the killer was just getting started. He laughed to himself at the thought, but his laughter seemed hollow now. It was a ghost's laugh. There was sadness in it.

It had no soul. Being shallow, though, Danny Rolex didn't spend much time contemplating what happens to a soul when one becomes a ghost. Or whether, when he was murdered, whether he even had much of a soul left. His primary concern was one of vanity. One of needing to know who would be so jealous of him that he would be seen as such a threat.

Danny had one clue to begin his search. That ugly scarf. He still wore a ghost form of the scarf about his neck, which wasn't really being worn as much as it was hanging, wrapped around him. If Danny could feel anything, it would still be too tight.

He moved through the partiers, sometimes moving literally through them.

Who could it be?

He had to know. He had been attacked from behind so he never saw who did it.

But it was an ugly scarf. Even uglier now in its spectral form in his estimation. Danny Rolex wondered if he would spend all eternity having to wear this… this abomination? This was not being a ghost, this was being in Hell itself.

As he moved through the crowd, he found himself judging each and every person there. No one was dressed the way he thought they should be. In Danny's eyes, they were fashion train wrecks, but as a ghost, he was grateful that he would no longer throw up at such sights.

This was terrible. And he feared that some of their ensembles might haunt him forever. He needed to leave. He needed to get away from his so-called friends, his fellow students, even before finding out the identity of the one who killed him.

He was so much better than any of them. And yet, they were living, and he was dead. It's the way of all geniuses, he thought as he passed them, leaving them and their mediocrity behind.

Perhaps if Danny had spent less time judging them, or less time thinking about himself, he might have seen that which had nothing to do with clothing.

Perhaps if Danny hadn't left when he did, he might not be a ghost any longer.

For the killer was there. And finding his killer would have allowed Danny to move on, to move beyond what he had been.

And that is the tragedy of the ghost that still walks the streets of the fashion district in New York.

Who still wanders begging the elements "why?" Not why he was killed, but why would anyone wear that?

Because if Danny had stayed, had thought longer and harder, he would have found one quiet student in the corner of the party with the tiniest hints of frostbite on his neck.

The smallest evidence that, on a cold, cold night like this, a certain killer shouldn't have given up his scarf.

To Ho Ho

Paris was aflame, its fine art was now burning.
And all the citizens had begun their pain-ed learning,
that there was no such thing as a safe hiding place
for any of those in this wine-sipping race.

It's sad now to say there's no more Mouline Rouge
No more bridge with love locks or even the Louvre.
The old churches in cinders, was that such a sin,
we all knew deep down that the creatures would win.

For the behemoths now, we knew they were coming,
But regardless it was, the cheese-eaters kept running.
They all certainly hoped that this was only a dream.
But who could even sleep through so many a scream?

And soon they saw as their skin started to blister,
they would have preferred that this be an earthquake
    or twister.
But fallout and gamma radiation are really real,
Which is why all they're skin was starting to peel.

The first to arrive was the king of all lizards,
The burning was 'nuff to retch all people's gizzards.
He towered above all the city's top towers,
While raining upon them radiated fire-blown showers.

'Twas the night 'fore Christmas when it dragged in
    the train,

But it wasn't folks' deaths that he had on the brain.
Only something that it knew that needed to be,
the train was the garland that would make up the tree.

So he wrapped it around, this unexpected choo-choo,
While the people within cried oh no and boo hoo.
The tower being wrapped was the famous Eifel,
Though it had never been a tree as any could tell.

But it needed so much more, and so it needed the Kong,
Monsters are monsters so what could be wrong.
The King did bring things that others would ape.
No matter how many Frenchmen wanted to escape.

The big monkey brought with him a number of cars,
Shoved into the tower, while the city was charred.
This monster exclaimed and enhanced all the frights,
while the tree was now glowing because of headlights.

And then came a monster with all kinds of stars,
It's possible this beast came down from the planet
    called Mars.
A pterodactyl to some, a god to yet others.
The tower was glowing, while it waited for brothers.

The three-headed gargantuan came with a fright,
But it didn't seem so bad, especially this night.
It brought with it tinsel in sparked telephone wire,
While now all calls for help would need far more than
    a plier.

Next the big moth flew in, having gathered its banners,
And wrapped round the tower showing rather
    unexpected manners.
The creatures all sat 'round their own special tree,
Waiting for one more they were excited to see.

The big turtle then came, flying down from the sky,
His shell was now glowing, he came down from high.

He came from some worlds beyond the known sky.
If the monsters were now here, he had the reason to
    why.

He's a friend to all children as you certainly know,
He's a very kind monster and had quite something to
    show.
Not as nearly as famous as reptile or ape,
He didn't bring things that would cause chests to now
    gape.

But that said, it is true that he sought his own part,
to reveal to these monsters what was left of their heart.
Perhaps it was lost to all in this fury,
Or maybe the fun of seeing all of us ants scurry.

He wanted to remind that monsters be not evil,
And dared even more than that stuntman Knievel.
Christmas was a chance to come out of a shell,
And protect all of those who feared the coming of Hell.

The tower became a gorgeous Christmas tree,
Though sacrifices you say were far more than should
    be.
They all had become the very worst of the most,
But that did not mean they could not share a holiday
    roast.

For monsters need Christmas like everyone else,
A time to stop screaming, a time for some bells,
A chance to hope this new year brings something
    of change,
From all those we are so very deranged.

And if there are those who feel bad now for Europe,
Man up my dear soul and get back in the stirrup.
For let the best of the past become the worst of the
    future,
And please now refrain from your justified stupor.

For now is the time to hope for the future,
So even the worst of us might become super.
For the past is the past of the times that have passed.
There's a new year to embrace and it's here now at
    last.

A Creature Was Stirring

I don't expect you to believe any of this. I have told myself repeatedly that it couldn't be, and I would know.

The reason you won't believe this, especially from me, is because I am the father of lies. I'm the Devil.

And someone has been stealing souls from me.

I'm sure you have your perceptions of me based on your upbringing or your movies or perhaps works of art that have shown me in all my greatness. I was an angel, you know, and like to believe that I still am one despite my burnt wings and a couple horns give or take.

It's not just the works of art that paint me as a bad guy, though.

But is it so wrong for me to have a say, is it so wrong for me to ask for a little empathy here? Maybe even, dare I request it, sympathy?

Think of the soul as a self-aware bag or sack. The way I like to work with souls is to encourage them to fill that bag with so many things that it stretches the seams of the bag so much so, that there's no room for love or family or even kindness. That to do such things would lead to the soul to fear that being vulnerable or kind or humble to another soul would risk the loss of everything that was already filling the bag. I encourage souls to protect themselves. At least until they come to me.

You see, like a lot of people, including comic book enthusiasts,

I'm a collector. Of course, when I receive a soul, it's never in so-called mint condition. In all cases, it's either well-worn or almost non-existent. But what's important to know, is that once someone hits the slab, their soul, their story, their unrequited wishes and dashed hopes and tarnished dreams and regrets, they're all mine.

Mine to play with. I'm the ultimate writer of fan fiction and I am a fan of every soul that comes to me. When you get here, I will be your biggest fan. And I'll probably have been waiting for a long, long time to get my hands on your story.

What can I say, life goes on.

Now the idea that anyone was taking parts of my collection away from me is a Hell of a thing to do. I'm sure you saw what I did there.

So where did the souls go?

I think that it's important to point out a few of the differences between me and you know who, the other guy.

God. Yeah, him.

First of all, we're not equal and opposite forces. I'm not the yang to his ying. He made me. I just didn't want to be what he wanted me to be. Is that so bad? I don't think so. And I wanted to give as many others the same opportunity to make the same choice as I did. And yes, to be fair, I get upset when they don't become what I want them to become. I get really upset. And mercy really isn't my thing.

See? I can be fair. You see that, right?

Where He can be everywhere at once, omnipresent being his word for it, I can't. Which is why I need my help. My informants. My flying monkeys if you will. They don't like to be called demons, but I don't see that changing anytime soon.

I also can't travel through time. But I can interact with an awful lot of the past, not just because I was there, but because of the many souls that are my guests here in Hell.

At any moment, I can interrupt any one of the stories that continue in this place. Every soul here, I imagine, would love a little interruption. Call it a moment for a station identification, or better yet, a word from the sponsor.

So having no access to the future and only access to the past,

I began to have my servants move through the ranks looking for any way to explain where these souls could be. Was there something in the past that escaped my sight? It's possible. I'm not perfect, you know. That's another difference between me and God. I'm willing to admit it. Or is that, if you'll pardon me a little joke, willing to confess it.

I went up to your world and began to search it for any possibility of a way to steal souls. I wanted to find out who would do such a terrible thing, and even why You-Know-Who would allow such a crime. He seems to allow an awful lot, but this seems unforgivable.

While I enjoy collecting souls and extending their stories, I can't say I'm much of a reader. Reading is a creative process that encourages the reader to imagine and create in their minds and hearts. Not for me. I'm not the creative type. I'm better at giving notes. And criticisms.

And so, there are those in my care who wish they weren't. Well, to be honest, and I can be that too, there really isn't anyone who loves being in my collection. But that's not the point. They're my collection.

And again, they were being taken from me.

I mentioned reading and books before because the answer came in the form of an author whose works were almost a hundred years old. His name was H.P. Lovecraft.

I went back home, back to my collection. Lovecraft never believed in anything but a void after mortality closed, so I knew he would be there.

When he wasn't, I was infuriated. And learned from a cell-mate that authors are difficult to keep in Hell. Perhaps it is because their books and their writings are extensions of their souls. It's another damnable way in which souls are like You-Know-Who. Acts of creation and all. An author's soul may indeed find its way here, but it hard to hold them for long. Especially if their works continue to be read. And Lovecraft's works, while I was delighted to find out were horribly depressing, also served to put a bit of the fear of God in those that read them. Which of course results in 'spiritual journeys' which are painful for all to endure. I was so angry with this answer that I had one of my demons rip the cell-mate's tongue out.

Was everyone becoming an author now? Is that why all these souls were stolen even before they entered my collection?

No. I'd be able to find these lost souls. And there are so many words being written that are never going to be read again.

I asked the cellmate to read to me one of Lovecraft's books. I had to wait for the cell-mate's tongue to grow back, of course. But time really isn't an issue for me.

Finally, I heard about a multi-tentacled beast called Cthulhu. It stirred from time to time, and when it did, it fed. It waited in another realm, and when a soul was on its way to me, which is a series of transitions from one state of being to another, Cthulhu consumed it. The book did not go into a lot of description about this 'stirring' and how long it lasted.

I learned from this book and others from the same author that there were beings older than me that fed upon souls. They fed upon every fear, wish, regret and hatred. Mostly they slept, which supports them being really old, but it doesn't matter.

They were stealing what was rightfully mine.

I screamed so loud that all of Hell could hear me. I wanted every soul to know how very upset I was.

My rage echoed through ancient caves and catacombs. It was heard in the various schools of Hell, where cruelty was mandatory and not an elective. It shook the awards that were displayed in the Hall of Fame of those with the greatest degrees of envy. It caused all those in murderers' row to even have a moment of appreciating the life of each other, which up till now, had been an impossibility.

There was no soul who did not hear my rage.

No soul that did not shudder and recoil in fear.

Except for one.

I heard his laughter first. There was someone here and he was laughing at me, which is something I could not bear. Laughter, as someone would say, is somewhat medicinal in its nature. So humor in Hell does not work, unless I am laughing at one of my souls. No one laughs but me. It would be like a boy scout making their own fire here. It's downright blasphemous. The laughter echoed against the echoes of my rage, and I heard other souls begin to giggle as well.

I went to the room where this rebellious laughter came from.

It was one of the older rooms, so it even took me awhile to get there. The elevator, if it is right to call it that, is organic, a living thing or series of things. The reality is that it's carried from one part of Hell to another by a multitude of hands that move the 'elevator' or 'Helevator' from one level to another.

But back to the insanity of who would dare laugh at me. The laughter belonged to someone I worked with many years before, a colleague for certain. But I had never heard him laugh before, at least nor here.

His name was Judas. And he laughed all the harder when I entered his home, which he had called a cell. This was something he told me a long time ago. But I never forgot that he had said this, and it still hurts. I guess I'm not a forgive and forget kind of guy. But you know, if he wanted a nicer place here in Hell, maybe he shouldn't have thrown away his silver. Smart.

Anyhow, there he was, and you know the worst of it? He didn't feel guilty about laughing at me at all. He had certainly felt guilty before. I had seen it. I had even encouraged it.

"This isn't Cthulhu," he said. "No one is eating souls. There is no creature on the verge of mortality hungry enough to consume us all."

If this was true, this was not good news. It meant that I was back to not knowing what had happened to the souls.

"Then where have my souls gone?" I asked Judas.

"They haven't gone anywhere, you idiot."

This was upsetting and Judas has no right to speak to me in this way. "Then what's happened?" I asked him.

"Christmas."

"Christmas? Jesus Christ you've got to be kidding. Christmas doesn't steal souls! People have forgotten all about that anyhow. It's an old story about a baby in a barn. And who even knows what a barn is anymore? Maybe people in Wisconsin.

But who wants their souls anyhow."

"Souls, given time, are changed by Christmas to such a degree that even you, Lucifer Morningstar, cannot recognize them anymore."

That's what the betrayer said. He even told me that he saw the Christmas baby here in Hell one day. He wasn't here for long, and he was an adult. But that's when Judas began to hope again. That's when he thought it would even be possible to laugh again.

I slammed the door on Judas at that point. I would hear no more of his lies.

The idea that a soul could be changed into something I can't even recognize, let alone collect, is a bigger lie than any I've ever told. No, there's a creature out there and it's feeding on us all. That's the only explanation that makes any sense. We all get hungry. We all eat more than we should, especially around the so-called Holidays.

Judas is trying to trick me.

Perhaps I should be impressed that he's learned so much over the thousands of years he's been here.

Naughty Town

He was a bad boy, and he knew it.

He was a bad boy, and he loved it.

His name was Logan Chesterton.

Perhaps the most surprising and redeeming aspect about Logan, though, was that he still loved his mother and father. Logan's behavior wasn't a rebellion against them, just everything else. He wanted to please them. He actually and without-a-doubt did love them. And he was surprised that they did not acknowledge and admire his unwillingness to be controlled by the so-called 'man' and society itself.

There was just something about being bad that seemed far more creative and therefore challenging. It was like his art. Something deep inside and quite complex that encouraged him to bend or break the rules. That somehow, the rules themselves were daring him to find a way, a creative approach or endeavor to both disrupt those so-called rules and redefine them.

That said, his parents wanted him to use his creativity in different ways, as parents must when there is a problem with their child.

So, it was not surprising when he learned that the family was moving from Michigan to an obscure town in North Alaska that his parents begged him to be good. To try to be the son that they knew he was. At least deep down, that they knew he was.

Times had been bad for the Chestertons and not only was the inheritance of a new house and the promise of jobs for both

Mom and Dad an incentive for the move, but the opportunity to give Logan the chance to start again with a brand new reputation with no record to be used against him. It was too good to be true.

Logan was ten years old and the town in Alaska was called Stokerton. Most cities are powered by various forms of electricity, like wind, solar and nuclear energy. This was a town that still ran primarily on coal.

There were legends as to why this was the case. But most never really bothered to remember them. What was important, antiquated though the town might be, was the fact that it worked for them.

There wasn't a parade for the Chestertons when they arrived. There was a small article on page three of the local newspaper, but that was it. But they thought it was nice that their arrival made the Stokerton Gazette.

They drove. It was a long trip, but they made it. There was even a time spent on a ferry with their car. Everything else was moved by vans, but most of their possessions were not even worth holding onto. There were no special collections, apart from a comic book run of X-Men written by Chris Claremont and drawn by John Byrne, and the series of Daredevil written and drawn by Frank Miller that mattered. Their furniture was worthless, as were their clothes. Though Michigan was cold in the winter, it wasn't Alaska cold for Fall, Winter and Spring. The trip to Alaska was not fast, and between packing, shipping and driving, it took over a month. It was Thanksgiving by the time they got there. And Thanksgiving wasn't like Thanksgiving everywhere else in America. It was more like a nice meal. And the chance to watch a parade in New York that was already over.

Black Friday was blacker than most Black Fridays, especially in Stokerton. In fact, daylight only lasted a couple hours because of how far north they were. And there would even be less daylight in the days to come as Christmas approached.

The first thing Logan Chesterton noticed about the city was how Mayberry it all seemed, except for the snow. It would be easy to skip a stone on the pond here, especially because it was frozen over so much of the year. In fact, to skip a stone here was to hit the other side of the lake, a place no one could even see.

It was known as a mining town and was about the size of one. If you've ever heard of Rico, Colorado, then you know, and you've also probably been there. That's not to diminish Rico, but also the recognition that you probably cannot diminish it because it is still so small as it is.

There was an advertising agency in Stokerton, Alaska and there was a factory that was also a forge. There was a diner. And a drug store that was also a grocery store. There was a hardware store. And a post office. There was one bar. The City Hall, which was small, was where Logan's mom and dad would start their jobs. Really, it was a small town. But a town of big secrets. All of which seemed to revolve around and be hinted at the diner in the breakfast hours which went to at least eleven, though breakfast was served all day.

It was the kind of town that Stephen King would write about the devil living in. Not just a devil, but THE Devil. But that's only if the devil was an insurance man, or in this case, an assurance man, therefore making certain that people went to hell and didn't have any last minute 'Hail Mary' salvations. It was a small town, as previously noted, and though Logan didn't know all the businesses that were there, it was enough for him to see what he could see.

Logan loved bubble gum. And, when finished, he loved spitting it on the sidewalk so that someone else would step in it. Again, this was just the briefest hint of Logan's 'art' and he justified such a thing by thinking that if someone got their gum stuck to their shoes, it meant that his genetic identity would be walked upon by others and they would just be spreading his mark all along the city which would have to speak to the reality that he was indeed here. If he was cursed for his bubba-yum-aliciousness, he would hear it as a compliment, and certainly not a chewing out.

So, he spit that gum high as he j-walked across the street. It arced up past the stop sign and came down to land perfectly, just a step outside the curb. He watched and waited for it to be stepped upon.

What he did not expect was the hand of an older man carrying an umbrella on his shoulder.

"Well done, Son. You're going to fit right in here."

The older man continued on his way, opening and closing his umbrella to upset the birds on the sidewalk, and Logan stepped up onto the other side of the street with a sense of both surprise and profound disappointment.

He still waited to watch someone step on his wad of gum, and someone did, shortly after. They swore, they shouted to the heavens and then seemed to move on into their day with more happiness to have sworn than to have stepped in gum.

Logan immediately knew there was something wrong with this town of Stokerton.

When he got home, to the new house which was really a very old house, his parents seemed very nervous that he might have done something wrong. But, of course, he denied anything at all. They then went on to talk about life in City Hall and all the new responsibilities they had.

Logan approached the next day with a certain trepidation. He began to pay more attention to the town. The people in the diner were simply rude. If there was an order for a plain hamburger, it was guaranteed to come with pickles and onions and a sauce which hadn't been refrigerated appropriately.

He learned that the manufacturing plant's sole purpose was to forge and assemble the boots that policemen put on cars to make certain that a car owner cannot drive the car and therefore get to where they want to get to.

There was an office building, and in that office building was an advertising agency. The agency's very purpose, though, was to write and produce anything in digital advertising that would be considered spam. If there was a virus that could be attached to the spam, they offered this service free-of-charge, but would accept tips for their hard work.

The pharmacy at the drug store also seemed to make certain

that it gave the wrong drugs to the wrong people. Not poisons, though. Just remedies that were not remedies and would make things worse before anything could be made better. And while they certainly would apologize, it would require hours in a separate line to return anything. The Rx in the sign seemed to suggest that going there was going to wReX your day. Which was true for everything in this town.

Logan decided to test this further.

There was an old woman who was standing in front of a bulletin board. She set her cane against the wall that the bulletin board had been secured to.

Logan didn't pay any attention to the announcements going on in the city, all of which were about events that did not seem right at all. Logan's focus was her cane, which he took while she was not looking.

He didn't laugh when she fell and was quite surprised when others did. When finally the doctor, who was actually a veterinarian, arrived and announced that she would need a new hip, the crowd cheered. She didn't really need a new hip. The doctor just said that in the hopes of upsetting her further.

Logan was not happy. This was crueler than anything he had ever done and the consequences of taking her cane were terrible. He wanted and wished that there had been a different result.

When he arrived home, he was greeted by parents who had heard great things about him and how much everyone in the town felt like he fit right in. They were relieved and they were proud.

He had never been so disgusted in his life. Fitting in is not what drove him. Or made him.

This was clearly a town that seemed to reward the doing of bad things. It was not a town for a creative person such as himself. So something had to be done. Something to get noticed. Something to break him from the congratulations and the head nods of affirmations that he was now receiving.

The next day, wanting to do something that would get some sort of rise from someone, he saw an old man crossing the street. The old man didn't use a cane, though he should have. Certain nerves didn't allow him the balance he once took for granted, but he was too proud to use a cane. Or a putter as he had tried to for a while.

No, the old man tried to cross the street, tried to get to the diner, and he fell.

To be honest, Logan did not run to help him up because Logan was trying to do something that would upset the town. He just did it because an old man had fallen and while Logan enjoyed being a bad boy, this was an old man and there was nothing funny about him falling. Especially in light of what he had done the day before.

Logan quickly realized that by helping the old man to his feet, the town was not happy at all. Not happy that he had done something… well, nice. They glared at him and whispered to each other. They shook their heads back and forth and scowled.

And it was in this action that Logan found his way. Rather than misbehave, his art would now be in doing good. To be kind and to do kindness would be his new way.

But while the entire town frowned at Logan's actions, Brin Briars, the granddaughter of the old man, smiled.

She made sure that she found Logan after school the next day.

"Hi. I'm Brin."

"I'm Logan."

"I liked what you did for my grandfather."

"And I like that no one liked that I helped him."

Brin smiled at this. She smiled because she knew, deep down, that this was not a town where people did good, and the fact that someone did, meant that he was a true rebel and was about to become Public Enemy Number One. Which meant she could become Public Enemy Number Two.

And so it began, Logan and Brin became thick as thieves. But it was a thievery that tried to steal away the cruelty of the town.

If there was gum on the ground, Logan would now scrape it up.

If someone needed help, they would help that person. If someone vandalized, they would rebuild and repaint that area to look better than it ever did before.

They said their "pleases" and they said their "thanks." Even a "you're welcome" was utilized from time to time. They honored all they met.

They visited the elderly in the nursing home, which was just an old apartment building. This was especially upsetting to a town that tried to ignore the old and treated them in a way that suggested that they had nothing to say at all. "If they can't hear us, why should we listen to them?" was the town model.

Logan and Brin began to collect cans and newspapers and other things from garbage bins and tried to set up a place where things could be recycled. The town really did not recycle before, other than to make each other eat from dirty plates.

And this behavior was drawing other kids from the school. Other rebels.

Doing kindness was becoming a virus that was infecting more and more children.

The mayor of Stokerton was Forrest Stoker. His family had been one of the very first families to settle here and it was their coal that kept the city going. There are other famous Stokers in the history of the world, including the one who wrote the greatest vampire story of all time. But there is no relation here.

Mayor Forrest Stoker's phone had not stopped ringing since Logan Chesterton helped that old man. There were lines of people waiting to talk with him and they were worried about their own children. They were worried about their own town.

And while Stoker prided himself on his willingness to have an open-door policy to all his fellow Stokertons, they were closing in on him all at once. And he was beginning to feel as if everything he had done to keep the town working, and keep their lives going, was in immediate danger. As if it was all caving in on him.

This would never do. So, he set up a meeting with Logan's parents. They worked at the City Hall and it was easy to arrange.

Logan's father was anxious to meet the mayor because as the city's new mechanical engineer, which was a fancier title than what he really was, had some questions. There was so much ash to clean up, coal to shovel, mechanisms to oil, and fires to keep burning to keep even a small town empowered.

Before coming to Stokerton he had indeed been an engineer but now felt more like a glorified custodian. But still, in his heart, it was good work to make sure everyone had power and warmth. It was good to know that his family had a home at last and that Logan had a new life and chance.

He was concerned, though, with how the town's furnace and heating system was an almost Frankensteined hodge-podge of steel, tin, wires and mesh. When something broke down, rather than get the right part to fix or modernize it, it was obvious that whoever had this job before simply used whatever was available to keep this monster going. And according to the city's newest engineer, Logan's father, the monster was on its last days. Which meant something would need to be done. By this point, even the right parts were not being manufactured anymore. And finding them was exceedingly difficult as they had long been considered antiques.

Logan's mother had been a city planner and was excited to meet with Mayor Stoker about her ideas for city expansion as well as enacting a promotion for tourism.

Both parents were heartbroken when they learned that the reason they sat across the desk of the mayor was because of their son, Logan.

"He's just not fitting in, and we had such high hopes for him," the Mayor told them. "He was one of the things that made your family so attractive to us."

"We have such high hopes for him, too, Mayor Stoker. We will take care of it and ask him to fit in better. Every culture is different, and I think that with a little patience, he'll figure it out. We all want to fit in here."

Logan's mother's words seemed to be what the Mayor wanted to hear. She didn't bother to ask exactly what Logan had done because she assumed that she and her husband had heard it all before.

The mayor suggested a job for Logan to help make things right and his parents heartily agreed, even believing this would be good for him and his sense of tradition and history regarding Stokerton.

The mayor thanked them for handling the problem that was their son and encouraged them to send him an email regarding their concerns about the city furnace and new ideas of how to make the city more efficient and welcoming to tourists.

Logan's parents went back to their respective jobs knowing that they had a rough night ahead of them. They were even a little surprised in their assumption that Logan had started to misbehave to such a degree, that it warranted a conversation with the mayor. They weren't surprised that it happened, only that it had happened so quickly.

Logan sat with Brin across the table from Brin's elderly grandfather. There was a story he had only ever told Brin, and she begged him to tell Logan. But knowing a story is different from remembering a story, and is different from telling a story.

Brin's grandfather began. "It might have been maybe 70 years ago. Forrest Stoker wasn't even born yet… His father… or maybe his grandfather… was mayor of Stokerton. It was as white a Christmas Eve as a Christmas Eve could be white. Everything was perfect. It was… perfect." Brin's grandfather began to stammer… and he started repeating himself. He stopped for more than a minute and coughed hard and long. Logan wondered if he was ever going to stop.

"My grandfather worked in the coal mines," she explained. "It wasn't good for his lungs and may even affect his memory." Logan sat concerned that the old man was going to die.

When he didn't die and was breathing better, the old man continued. "We were decorating for Santa's arrival, but then the generator broke down… Broke down…" The old man began to cough again. The story wasn't going to be told. That was clear.

Brin helped her grandfather lay down on his old day bed.

And they left.

"Santa?" Logan asked. "Really?" Logan was from one of those families that didn't believe in Santa, so his parents bought him gifts.

Who is to say that, perhaps if Logan DID believe in Santa before coming to Alaska, he might not have worked so hard to get on the 'Naughty List'. That said, he, of course, didn't believe in a 'Naughty List' either.

Logan, forgetting for a moment that he wanted to do good now, couldn't stop laughing.

Brin pushed Logan away. "I thought you were different."

Logan went home. Alone. And wished he would have apologized. Wishing he could have apologized was something new to Logan. He didn't want to say he was sorry to even get attention. Or do something right to get noticed. No, he really wanted to just say it. Because he felt like he was wrong.

This was new.

When Logan reached home, his parents were waiting for him. He tried to tell them how crazy this town was. How when he did something bad, the town congratulated him. And when he finally did something good, for the first time in a long time, the city acted like he was Public Enemy Number One.

Logan's parents were used to Logan lying, so it was not their fault that they did not believe him. And even more, regardless of his record, the idea of a town punishing a person for doing good, being polite, or helping a neighbor? Who would believe that from even the best of children?

Logan was told of the job awaiting him, his chance to show the Mayor and the people of Stokerton that he would try to fit in.

Logan reluctantly agreed, hating but accepting with some revelation the fact that he couldn't be trusted.

The job was this. He was to go to the Stoker Coal Mine and get the latest reading and estimations of expected coal consumption for the next three months. It was going to be a long winter and it was necessary to know how far the town would have to keep digging to ensure the warmth and energy of the town after the New Year arrived.

Logan wondered why, if the Mayor was so upset with him, he would be sent on a mission intended to help the town. You would think that in a place like this, such an act would be helpful and therefore hated. That if anything, he should throw a stink bomb in there or something. That's what it seems they wanted him to do.

On the way he thought about Brin. And he thought about Santa. He had always made fun of kids that believed in ol' Saint Nick. But he hadn't felt bad about it before. He hadn't felt a number of things before. The truth was that he liked being good. When he got back from the mine, he planned that he would stop at Brin's and apologize. Yes, apologize.

"Logan!" A voice called out.

He turned to see Brin catching up to him, trudging through the snow.

It was awkward, what he first said, but he wanted her to know that he was sorry.

"It's okay. No one really takes my grandfather seriously anymore."

Logan smiled. "I think that's the complete opposite of okay."

They continued down the frozen path. This really wasn't the way either of them wanted to spend the two days before Christmas. It was a long walk to the mine.

"Can you tell me the story your grandfather was trying to tell? I promise I won't laugh at the Santa part."

"Really?"

"Well… I promise I'll try not to."

"Pinky?"

"Not sure I want to take my mittens off in this weather, but yeah, pinky promise."

"Okay, well the way my grandfather tells it, the whole town was preparing for Santa's arrival. Because it was always so dark, the lights of our town were especially important. And we lit the town for his arrival. And then, when the lights on the Christmas tree were plugged in, something of a short happened. And all the lights went out. So Santa was never going to come because he couldn't see through the smoke, clouds, and the cold that evening. The town was going to freeze and die if it were not for old man Stoker. He used his coal furnace to save the town. And so, we have depended on coal every year since."

Brin explained how the town became crueler and crueler. Stokerton became a place where Santa seemed to turn a blind eye. Where he didn't bother to pay attention to the sleeping or the awake. Or the pouting or the doubting.

And things turned naughty. Naughty for naughtiness' sake.

Multiple times during their talk-n-walk, Logan looked over his shoulder. He was convinced that someone was following them, but who would? And whenever he turned, there was no one there. He couldn't see that well, though, because of the cold and wind. And because it was getting darker and darker. He had been told by his parents that the mine was only an hour's walk away, but it was already more than two hours.

Logan and Brin reached the mine, finally, and were surprised that there was no one at the entrance to greet them.

Assuming that the miners they were searching for were further into the cave, they headed in, and soon became aware of a strange hissing noise behind them. This also didn't make sense because Alaska, even in caves or mines, is not known for its indigenous snake population.

It wouldn't be until after the explosion that the dust and an almost-eardrum-popping echo that was followed by a cave-in, that Logan and Brin realized that there had been an explosion. The hissing was a wick being burned to the core.

This was so much worse than the stink bomb idea Logan had had earlier. They could have been killed.

They… were supposed to be killed. There had been someone behind Logan. There was someone following them. And that person certainly intended for harm to come to them.

The thought was heavy for both, and finally Logan told Brin

that it wasn't intended for her. No one knew she was going to be here. This was all about Logan. Someone wanted him dead. Maybe the whole town did. But that didn't seem right, either. So then, who would do this?

This was evil, not just naughty.

Forest Stoker approached the home of the Chestertons with a piece of paper in his gloved hand. He looked behind himself as he walked, not because he expected anyone to be there, but to see how deep his tracks were. The snow was falling so hard, that some of his tracks were already well on their way to being filled.

As for the paper, it was a 'Goodbye' note that was 'left' at the City Hall. It was from Logan.

Mr. and Mrs. Chesterton read the note and were surprised to hear that their son, Logan, had decided to run away from home. The note explained that when he got to the coal mine, it was caved in. And feeling like nothing could undo the harm he brought to Stokerton, it would be better for everyone if he left.

The Chestertons were horrified. And they blamed themselves for Logan's departure. Mayor Stoker tried to console them and remind them that this didn't mean their son wouldn't return to them.

But they feared differently. And didn't even think about the job that the Mayor had sent Logan on, or why the Mayor didn't show concern for the miners as well.

They set out into the winds and falling snow in hopes that they would find their son. Not just because they didn't want him to run away, but because this was no weather to be outside in. No weather to be trapped in. They feared for his life. It was now Christmas Eve. And the snow was not going to stop anytime soon.

The mine was old and seemed abandoned. That's the first thing that Logan noticed. And while there was dust everywhere, it did not look like it had been walked through for a very long time.

"Do you see any minors?" he asked.

"No," said Brin with some surprise.

The cave was empty.

And no one had been here in a very long time.

It was coal-less.

"But I don't understand, the town has always... Where's the coal?" she said, trailing off, her words echoing like dead stones skipped into the far reaches of this place.

There was no light to be found apart from what their cell phones could generate, and even then, their batteries were not full.

They turned off any kind of location services because they knew that no one would be able to find them in the mineshaft. There were no calls that could be made. No chance, especially in the snow, that they would be found. And there was no way to dig themselves out after the cave-in. Their only hope was another entrance. Another way out than the way they had come in.

Logan's father wanted to stay out longer than he did. Logan's mother insisted on it. But when they got to the cave, and saw it was indeed caved in, and covered in snow. There was nowhere else to search in any direction they tried to look. Whatever tracks they thought that Logan might have gone in were now covered with snow, wiped clean by the storm.

Both of Logan's parents were crying and their tears were freezing on their cheeks well before reaching the bottom of their faces. If they had tried to wipe these tears from their faces, it would have resulted in scratches and maybe even scarring.

Defeated, and with only the smallest whiff of hope, which isn't much, they made their way home, and even that was a torment. Even their breathing hurt.

Sometimes people feel lost at Christmastime, and sometimes those who are not lost still feel a lostness because of what's happening in the lives of those they care for. This is the terrible woe of Christmas. This is the sadness that comes with loving others. The despair one feels for a brother or a sister, or of a son or a daughter, or a friend. It is the powerlessness that comes with being human.

Sometimes hope is all that's left.

There was a minecar that Logan and Brin came upon in the blackness of the empty coalmine. Their phones' batteries were almost dead when they found the car. Their light was dimming. As was their hope. And they feared the worst. They climbed into the cart, knowing that the worst would soon befall them.

"If I die first, I want you to know that it's okay if you eat me," said Logan. "But make a fire so I don't look like me if you must eat me. I'm sure I'll taste better that way and maybe even look better."

"And if I die first, you can eat me," said Brin. And then, with a smile, she said, "and I think I'm sweeter, so it's probably better if I get eaten first."

"But I'm spicey." Logan joked. Then, after a hesitation, he continued. "I'm sorry I got you into this. I'm sorry, again, that I laughed about your grandfather. I would like it if there really was a Santa. I would like it if I had been wrong all this time about things."

"Let's be honest," she replied as the light went out completely. "There was no room for us in Stokerton. There was no room for kindness." And with that she kissed him. It was the first kiss for both. And she was lucky to find his lips in the dark.

The minecar began to move moments later. It started slow, but it didn't stay that way. It accelerated in the dark, moving down sometimes and then up, turning on its side, sometimes only two wheels on the track.

Logan and Brin screamed. Time lost all meaning. And it was cold. Maybe even colder than it had been outside. What direction were they even going? It also made no sense that time seemed to slow while they accelerated. If this was a roller coaster, they would have loved it. But that wasn't what this was. Clearly, because of the speed, they were either to fly off the tracks, or to hit a wall. They were going to die. On Christmas Eve.

They were going to die.

But they didn't. They had stopped almost as quickly as they began and there was light. At first they sighed a terrible relief. And then a grateful one. And then they thought about that kiss and didn't look at each other. And when they finally did, they started looking around. And began to note where they were. It was the end of the cave.

There was a stairway in front of them. It was a winding one, a spiral one that led up out of the mine. Between the stairs there was what looked like a fireman's pole.

Logan took her hand. In the moment it reinforced that kiss. But they kept moving upward wondering how long they had been in the cart or on that ride.

They never imagined what they would walk up into.

It was Santa's Toy Factory. The pole in the center of the spiral staircase was actually the North Pole. It wasn't for sliding down at all, but for marking the top of the world.

They were surrounded by elves still finishing up toys this Christmas Eve. The last-minute wrapping of gifts was happening as quickly as some toys were being finished. The elves had pointy ears. And were quite small. And there were many as well. They stopped their work when Brin and Logan stepped up into their workspace. And then immediately went back to work, as if it didn't matter that Logan and Brin were there at all.

And then they heard the laugh. At first it hurt their ears, like a sub-woofer turned up to the maximum would result in. They felt it in their feet first. And it moved up into their stomachs.

They laughed at the laugh. They laughed because it seemed impossible. It was so deep. And so loud. It smelled of cookies.

The best cookies. And of chimneys. And of nuts. And maybe even eggnog. Surely, this was the smell of the breath that came with the laughter.

The entire factory seemed to echo this laugh. The elves laughed too as they finished their last gifts and their last wrappings.

It was Santa.

It was the worst of situations. But there he was, still laughing as if he were in on a joke that suggested that no matter how bad things were, there was still a reason for joy. That no matter how dark a Christmas was, there was reason to laugh.

There was something deep inside Logan that began to make itself to the surface. It was a laugh as well. It was a revelation. That Christmas was a way to laugh at the cruelty of the world in a way that diminished it. To mock it. It was a defiance. The kind of defiance that Logan always, deep down, knew to be true. Maybe the defiance that encouraged Logan to behave, not only the way he did before coming to Stokerton, but the defiance that led him to do good as well.

Brin smiled, and laughed as well, as Santa came to them laughing and so happy to see them. He was used to visiting children and was overjoyed to have these two visit him.

He was not as hefty as they had expected. He was more like a warrior, a barbarian of sorts. He had a cane, and it wasn't a candy one. It steadied his walk as he came closer. Logan imagined that his limp was the result of a great battle he had fought and won.

Logan started to speak but Santa stopped him.

"Sometimes the burning of coal and the grey clouds obscure even my vision. Just ask Mrs. Clause."

"So, it's like your Kryptonite?" asked Brin. Logan was impressed by her question and her understanding of Superman.

"I love Superman. I fear for a world that embraces Batman more. Though both heroes are great," Santa said. Santa. I wanted to swear. It was so cool. But now I was, for the first time, truly aware of the Naughty List.

We asked him about Stokerton, realigning our story with

him. And asked what was going on.

"I see clearly now, finally," he repeated himself. "When the electric generator broke down and the Stoker family got the old coal furnace going again, they realized that they needed coal to keep the city going. They needed more than the old mine, which was already almost empty, could offer."

Brin thought about her grandfather's stories. Logan was already putting two and two together to equal what all the naughty of Stokerton was there for.

"Are you telling me, Mr. Santa?"

"Just Santa."

"Okay, but are you telling me that this town, Stokerton, over all these years, was being naughty just to get enough coal from you to keep their lights and heat on?"

"Yes."

Santa started laughing again.

"That's so stupid," Logan said.

Santa laughed more. "Yes, it is. People often do cruelty in the hopes that it will make something better. They lie in the hopes that it will result in something it could never result in. They steal in the hopes that what they take will be nothing compared to what they give. They cheat on each other in the hopes that the hollow furnace within them will be warmed by such false coal."

Brin asked if he could help the town of Stokerton even if they didn't deserve it.

Santa, with a smirk, asked what kind of a question that was to even ask him. He smiled and reminded them both that he was Santa.

It was Christmas, after all. And nothing was better than Christmas.

Santa arrived in Stokerton with both Brin and Logan. They came in from the sky on a sleigh being pulled by nine reindeer. It's important to note this because we so often take it for granted. The flying reindeer pulled the sleigh. And a certain self-illuminating reindeer, who is so much more than the song about him, needed to work harder than he ever had before. This wasn't just fog. This wasn't just bad holiday weather. It was the dankest, darkest, most terrible pollution one could possibly consider. Every part of him, including his nose, felt dirty as he lit their way to and through the clouds and sky on the way to Stokerton.

On the ride Santa had explained that part of how he was able to deliver all the presents to all the kids in all the world was something of a time loop. It was this same time loop that Brin and Logan had entered on the minecar ride to the North Pole.

He also told them what he was going to do.

Perhaps it was still just that whiff of hope that allowed Logan's parents to see Santa's sleigh before anyone else in town did that early Christmas morning. Or maybe it was a dream, one they both shared, and one that was coming true. Again, this was Christmas.

As they arrived, the town was amazed. In the past, the coal had just been dumped outside of town and they never saw Santa himself.

But they saw him now. And they saw Brin and Logan with him.

Mayor Forest Stoker had heard the stories about Santa. He had heard them from his father, and from his father's father. He knew that Santa had seen him. After all, Santa saw all. There are certain customs that say that to see all is to forgive all, but this was not the mindset of the mayor of Stokerton.

He had been found out.

He was the one who wrote the 'running away' note that was taken to the Chestertons. Santa now saw it. He was the one that threw dynamite into the tunnel. That was something, too, that Santa could now see. It was him, trying to make certain that the status quo of the town remained what it had been.

His family had kept this naughtiness lifestyle intact, from generation to generation, always keeping enough cruelty to get enough coal to warm the town. But Forest had taken it further when he tried to kill Logan, and therefore Brin, unknowingly.

He ran into the snow, away from the town. He ran as hard and as far as he could, but Santa reminded Brin and Logan that there was nowhere he could go that Santa could not see. And promised that Forrest would get what he deserves. In other words, as Mayor of Stokerton, he was about to be sacked. But that has more to do with Santa's Krampus than Santa himself.

For the town of Stokerton, Santa brought a new furnace, like the one he used at the North Pole. It was a perpetual heater, a light source and power station that ran on snow, of which there was always an ample supply.

Santa explained to the town that the bringing of coal was supposed to be a good thing. It's a diamond in the rough. As are all the people he ever brought coal to. They weren't fully formed into the person and being of value that they were supposed to be. And he was sad that this town never became more.

But they promised that they would. And this was enough for Santa because sometimes, being changed by Christmas, it takes a while.

In time, the town turned into a place of beauty, kindness, and warmth again. Logan's mom became the new Mayor, and Logan's father became one of the most beloved people in town, always giving everyone more than a second chance.

Once kindness, though, became the new rule of Stokerton, now called Diamondtown, Logan wondered what he would do to get noticed.

While thinking about this, he unwrapped a new piece of bubble gum.

Haunted House Arrest

We always remind each other that it's best to be home for the holidays. After all, home is where the heart is. Though, to be honest, some holidays that we experience with the extended family feel a little like being a prisoner. A little like a sentence that seems like it's never going to end.

This makes December 26th a glorious release from the good behavior of the few days prior.

But the people who say this have no idea what prison is really like. Or what it's like to have an ankle monitor, also called a tether, forcing you to stay in one place. In one location.

They have no idea what it would mean to have the freedom to just be able to walk to the neighborhood store and buy a soda. Or a pack of gum. Or even a roll of toilet paper.

To be fair, house arrest is still so much better than prison. But it is a prison, and maybe no more so than on Christmas. When even your friends, those who visit on a regular basis to watch movies or bring food, are invited to their families and to other parties, and feel the need to explain their absence with words like "It's only once a year," or "We'll be back in a couple more days."

This was not my house. I didn't have a permanent residence, so this house was used for those under house arrest that didn't have a house.

It also came with a ghost. His name was Henry. I knew this because he told me so but really didn't say much else. He also seemed to always be there.

This ghost, that was in my house, was especially frustrating. I had to chase him out of the bathroom many times. It made everything more difficult. Or maybe I should just eat more dried fruit. I don't know. Maybe he just missed the most basic experiences of humanity. And don't even ask me about the bedroom.

I asked him about his story and he said nothing. Nothing. He had a story. We all do. But it was more like he didn't know where to begin and that, therefore, affected how he would end his story. And so, without a beginning or an ending, he just didn't say anything. Sad. Haunted. He was trapped in lost scenes without a spine or thread. Maybe that's what it's like for ghosts. Not to see your story. To not see how it all holds together. How it's tethered.

So why was I under house arrest? I bought a used car that turned out to be a stolen car. The seller was really, really good at covering his tracks. Or is that treads? I bought something that wasn't mine to buy. I owned up to something that wasn't mine to own. And I didn't know the interest that would accrue.

Anyhow, here I was, on Christmas, in a home in Idaho that was already furnished. There was a storm outside. The streaming services, in fact almost everything related to any kind of outside messaging, was facing a lot of interference.

While I tried to get an old VHS machine working, because there were tapes here, the electricity went out. All I had was a fireplace, candles, and what was already in the house.

I noticed a bookshelf filled with books. All of them seemed to be horror-related in one way or another. But also, they were Christmas inspired. Not in a sappy way at least. Not in a feel-good way.

There was one about a monster, a manufactured creature, that was made up of toys. Another that was a sort of prequel to *A Christmas Carol* where the ghost of Jacob Marley tried to save his old partner on the brink of death. And another that, in a storm, had been about a city that was wiped out by snow forever. There were stories of werewolves, vampires, and evil elves. Cannibals, a Krampus, and a Reindeer's ghost. Even a gnarly sock that was transformed into a Christmas stocking.

I read these stories and was frustrated, even angry, because they did not speak to the Christmas I wanted them to. Many were sad and ironic. Not the Christmas I thought they were supposed to be. But it got me thinking about stories.

At one point in my life, I had wanted to be a screenwriter. And the idea of being under house arrest in a haunted house seemed like a perfect pitch. A perfect supernatural comedy about a guy trapped with ghosts, none of which could leave. An exorcist movie with no exit in sight. Green and red puke mixed in a happy 'how that would twist the mind and head of any movie goer…'

It would be great.

It would be evergreen money for me.

But not this. Not this story. Henry just stood there. Like an idiot. A would-be witness to nothing. He just stood there. Watching. Looking to me for some kind of answer that I could not offer him. As far as the books went, I did not want stories of being alone. Being without. Being changed. Being reminded of the past. Being forced to see the future. Becoming a monster. Or a lost ghost. Not that.

There were no other options than these stories on the shelf. No choice but to see the Christmas that they suggested.

Their Christmas was sad. But still glad. It was dark, but not without the promise of another day. And while there was good will towards man, it was also a sort of last will and testament to the entire race as it had been. Sort of the death of the world that was, until Christmas brought something new.

Rather than peace on Earth, it was about the pieces we find ourselves in. The brokenness of the world, of God, and of life.

Instead of 'not a creature was stirring,' there were many creatures here and they were all stirring. All groaning under the weight of the reality that they were monsters.

Forget a silent night. These stories brought noise and troubles. And sometimes there wasn't a star to light the way, to follow, or even to wish upon.

Pinocchio's desire to become a real boy, to have real life, was also a death. A death of immortality for the sake of a greater mortality.

I don't want to die.

I want to live. At least I said I did. But did I really?

And maybe that was what these stories spoke to. Life. New life. One that was just beginning, but still emerging from the old one. The pains of new birth. The pains of old death.

I looked at Henry the ghost many times while I read these stories, all of them to candlelight. There was a flicker to them, every word re-illuminated as if it was meant to haunt further. A spiritual strobe of sorts.

Henry didn't say anything. I asked him again and again for some kind of an answer as to why these stories were here. But he couldn't say anything. It was like he didn't understand the question. We both spoke English, but it was as if we did not.

And then it occurred to me. I was not trapped here. He was. I would leave this place one day. One day soon. He could not.

My past. My story. My experiences. They would be left behind me, whereas his would not. They were only a part of my story but not my entire story. He was trapped in his as were all ghosts who refused to move on. Move forward onto their next chapters.

I could move on. I would move on. I would live.

And he would not.

Perhaps, those of us who are haunted are lucky. We are fortunate to be stuck in the past, for a moment, no matter how long that is, and still see a future waiting for us. A future welcoming us.

Lucky to see that there is a tomorrow. A day after Christmas. Not just the day before. Fortunate enough to see a New Year coming.

Perhaps being haunted is what it's all about.

Haunted.

And still able to be grateful to be so.

Biographies

(in order of appearance)

Cover Artist/Internal Art, JOHN K. SNYDER III

John K. Snyder III is an Eisner-nominated Illustrator and writer of comic books and graphic novels. Creator of the independent comic series *Fashion In Action*, and adapter/illustrator of the graphic novel adaptation of Grand Master mystery writer Lawrence Block's classic novel *Eight Million Ways to Die*, published by IDW. He has worked for nearly every major publisher, including DC, Dark Horse, Marvel, IDW, and many others. Snyder worked on *Suicide Squad* during its classic 1980's run with writers John Ostrander and Kim Yale, and provided covers for the 2007 Suicide Squad mini-series and Suicide Squad covers coinciding with the release of the 2021 James Gunn movie. Along with Matt Wagner, Snyder co-created the Pieter Cross version of *Doctor Mid-Nite* for DC and *Lady Zorro* for Dynamite. Snyder also worked with Wagner on the epic *Grendel: God and the Devil* storyline. John has also illustrated covers for author Jim Krueger's renowned *Foot Soldiers* comics series and is delighted to be working with Jim once again on this book. Find him at http://www.johnksnyder.com and as @johnksnyder3 on Instagram and Threads, @JohnKSnyderIII1 on Twitter, and John K Snyder III on Facebook.

Author, JIM KRUEGER

Jim Krueger is the former Creative Director of Marvel Comics and a *New York Times* best-selling author, best-known for his work on iconic comic book titles such as *Earth X*, *Justice*, *Avengers*, *Star Wars* and more. He has written for some of the biggest publishers in the business, and collaborated with industry heavyweights like Alex Ross, Gerard Way, Steve Aoki, Sam Raimi, Bill Sienkiewicz and John Paul Leon. In addition to his work in comics, Jim has written for film, television, and video games, contributing to projects such as the *Spider-Man 2* video game, *Mortal Combat* and the animated series *Justice League*, among others. A visionary creator, Jim's ideas about world-building have been a major influence in shaping popular culture through comics, TV, and film. His groundbreaking *Earth X* trilogy, which was awarded Best Series of the Year by *Wizard Magazine*, became the basis for much of the Marvel Universe continuity, influencing movies and TV shows such as *Fantastic Four*, *Blade*, *Black Panther*, *Eternals*, *Moon Knight*, *Captain Marvel*, and *Loki*. For Warner Brothers, Jim's stories and consulting have influenced everything from *Batman* to *Justice League* and to *Harley Quinn* and the *Suicide Squad* movies.